Holme Lee

The Wortlebank Diary - And Some Old Stories from Kathie Brande's

Portfolio

Vol. I

Holme Lee

The Wortlebank Diary - And Some Old Stories from Kathie Brande's Portfolio
Vol. I

ISBN/EAN: 9783337047573

Printed in Europe, USA, Canada, Australia, Japan

Cover: Foto ©Andreas Hilbeck / pixelio.de

More available books at **www.hansebooks.com**

THE

WORTLEBANK DIARY,

AND SOME OLD STORIES FROM

KATHIE BRANDE'S PORTFOLIO.

BY HOLME LEE,

AUTHOR OF "SYLVAN HOLT'S DAUGHTER," ETC.

IN THREE VOLUMES.

VOL. I.

LONDON:
SMITH, ELDER AND CO., 65, CORNHILL.
M.DCCC.LX.

CONTENTS

OF THE FIRST VOLUME.

ADVERTISEMENT.

In the WORTLEBANK DIARY, which is entirely new, I
have set, as in a framework, many OLD STORIES;
some of these have appeared in *Household Words*
and the *National Magazine*, and are reprinted by
the kind permission of Mr. CHARLES DICKENS and
Messrs. KENT.

THE

WORTLEBANK DIARY,

AND SOME OLD STORIES FROM

KATHIE BRANDE'S PORTFOLIO.

From the Diary.

Wortlebank Rectory,
December 10, 18—.

JUST before Felix set off this morning to go to the clerical meeting at Bowerham, he came into my dressing-room, with a rather solemn face, and said,—

"Kathie, there is my curate giving Emmy another lesson in botany in the shrubbery."

"Well, Felix," replied I; "and botany is a very pleasant and profitable study."

"But do you consider this the sort of weather

for it? There cannot be many flowers or even weeds out on the 10th of December."

"I assure you, Felix, I saw a primrose peeping up in the moss yesterday."

"And Emmy's primroses are beginning to peep too, I suppose?" He came and sat down opposite to me at my writing table, and added more seriously, "You like Mr. Dover, Kathie?"

"Yes, Felix, I do. There is everything about him to like."

"And you think Emmy and he have taken a fancy for each other?"

"I am sure of it; and the botany lessons were the beginning of it."

"Then what would you do?"

"Nothing."

That was every word which passed between us on the subject at that time; for I am a great enemy to premature meddling with young folks' affairs. Felix left me in a reflective mood, and went downstairs; a minute or two after I saw him drive down the avenue, and pick up Mr. Dover at the gate. I knew that Emmy's botany lesson must be for the present at an end, and in about a quarter of an hour, she made her appearance in the dressing-room. I saw that her mind was preoccupied, so I took little notice of her, but went on with my letter to my sister, Jean Maynard, until I felt the dear child's hand softly laid on my shoulder, and her voice, with a trembling in it, saying,—

"Mamma, I have something to tell you."

Of course I understood in a moment, and held her close clasped in my arms, until the little palpitation was over, when she sat down, rosy and happy, and asked me what I thought papa would say.

"Mr. Dover is to speak to him as they come home from Bowerham," she added.

"Mr. Dover had better have relieved his mind as they went to Bowerham," said I; "I would not give much for his wisdom at the meeting with such a weight on it, if one of the difficult Daniel prophecies comes up for discussion."

"He is not obliged to talk, mamma; you know papa often says how hard it is to get a word in when Mr. Close and Mr. Sharpe are there."

Every little sentence was concluded with a sigh of over happiness; so as soon as I had finished my letter to Jean, with a riddle in the postscript for her to guess, I proposed to Emmy that we should take a long, sunshiny walk, to calm our minds. We only returned just in time for the two o'clock dinner which, when Felix is absent at the clerical meetings, Emmy and I sit down to, with Belle and her governess, Miss Mostyn. On these occasions we have our dessert spread on the round table in the drawing-room, and the event partakes of the character of a holiday; especially it did to-day, for there was a general tone of satisfaction pervading our atmosphere, and it is my belief that both my little daughter and Miss Mostyn guess what has come to pass. But we were not talkative; and Emmy's eyes had a far-away, happy look, as if her thoughts had gone to the clerical meeting.

She is, I am glad to think, a very sunshiny, even-tempered creature, and will make a delightful wife. Within the last year she has grown quite womanly; gentle, gracious, and blooming. If I wanted to describe her to a stranger who had never seen her, I should say that she was my ideal of a "Fair Woman." And she has great good sense as well as beauty. There is as much affection and confidence between us to the full, as there could have been were we own mother and daughter. My dear little Belle does not trust me more than Emmy always did, or love me better; and amongst the children themselves there has never been the smallest jealousy. When they are all at home together, I think Wortlebank must surely be the happiest spot in the universe! Harry and Steenie get up little amicable squabbles now and then, as to the respective merits of Rugby and Westminster; but both the lads are a credit to their school. We expect great things since Harry has taken such a high degree, and I should not think it at all beyond Steenie's merits if he announced himself captain when he came home for his Christmas.

We sat over our nuts and oranges so long, that blind man's holiday stole upon us unawares; and Belle, upon whom the silence even of content sits heavily, renewed a petition to me, which she has often made before; this petition is, that during the winter twilights I will allow that old portfolio of mine, which was so long in my sister Jean's possession, to disburthen itself of its secrets —namely, the stories and sketches I used to amuse myself with writing when I was Kathie Brande— for I have added but little to them since Felix and I were married.

Emmy pressed the request, too.

"We will take our turn at reading aloud," said she; "and Miss Mostyn is a beautiful reader."

"Come, mamie, do," pleaded Belle, coaxing, with her arm round my neck.

I said I would think about it, upon which little Miss Wilful, who takes after her father in her steady pertinacity of getting her own way, told me that, "Procrastination was the thief of Time;" and appealed to Miss Mostyn if her copy-slips did not say so.

"Run away then," replied I, giving my hasty permission. "You will find the portfolio on the top shelf of my wardrobe."

Belle was not long before she returned, balancing it on her crown, and asking,—

"Mamie, did you make all this really out of your own head? It must be ever so much lighter now than it was, if you did." And then she let it fall with a crash on the floor, the strings broke, and the contents flew far and wide over the carpet. Both Emmy and Miss Mostyn sprang to help her to gather them up, but Belle spread herself out over them, exclaiming,—

"Nobody is to touch them but me! I elect myself custodian of the portfolio forthwith, and I shall choose each day what is to be read."

We none of us much care to interfere with Belle, when she gets into the imperative mood about trifles, so she was tacitly allowed to re-arrange the papers in their receptacle, and decide on what we should have; fortunately for her, each sketch and story was tied up with penny ribbon in a bunch by itself, so she had only to lay them straight again. As she did so, she read out the titles, made her remarks, and asked her questions.

"Is there much love and stuff in them, mamma?" was one of her inquiries.

"Well, my dear, I am afraid there is," re-

turned I. "Try a short one first, and then if
you repent of what you have undertaken, you
know it is very easy to carry the portfolio back
to its hiding place."

"This is a short one, 'Kester's Evil Eye,' and
I rather like the name. 'Founded on Fact.' Oh,
mamie, now is that a polite little literary fiction?
You have to confess."

"It is founded on fact, Belle, really and truly,"
I assured her, with due solemnity.

"That is satisfactory, for I like things real
best. Now, Miss Mostyn, you shall enjoy the
honour of reading first, and when I have lit the
little green lamp, which is all I propose to allow
during these twilight recreations, I shall make
myself comfortable in papa's chair. Read up,
please, and give all the provincial words the
proper twang. Mamie, you are going to have
your lamb's-wool knitting, and Emmy and I will
sit in judgment. Now, Miss Mostyn, you may
begin; and nobody is to speak until the tale is
finished."

KESTER'S EVIL EYE:

A STORY FOUNDED ON FACT.

———◦◇◦———

I.

In the cottage to the left hand of the forge at Harwood there lived, about five and twenty years ago, a man of the name of Christopher—or, as the country-folks abbreviated it, Kester—Pateman. He had formerly held the post of village blacksmith and farrier, but had long since retired from the exercise of his craft. He was said to have the gift of the evil eye; not that he was a malicious man, but that involuntarily his look blighted whatever it fixed upon. Friend or enemy, his own children or aliens, it was all one; Kester's eye settled on them, and they withered away. No single thing prospered with him. The crops on his little farm were always either frosted, blighted, or miserably thin; or, if they were good and abundant, rain came after the corn was cut, and it lay out until it sprouted and rotted away; once he got it all stacked, and the stack took fire; another time the grain was threshed out and stored up in safety, but the rats devoured a third of it. His cattle were the leanest in the country; his sheep died of disease; his children perished one by one as they grew up to manhood and womanhood; every horse he shod fell lame before it had gone a mile. Kester was a miserable man; all the country avoided him as if he had got the plague.

Kester had one child left: a daughter, born long after the rest; she being the offspring of a young Irish girl, whom he had chosen to marry in his old age. The Irish girl ran away soon after the child's birth, on the plea of having a husband in her own country, whom she liked better.

Kester made no attempt to bring her back, but contented himself with spoiling Katie. Katie was not a bit like what his other children had been; she was her mother over again. Two wide-opened, dark blue eyes, a white skin considerably freckled, black elf locks, always in a tangle, a wide red mouth, and little teeth like pearls; a figure smart and lissome, and a step that lilted along as if it kept time to an inward tune, made of Katie a village beauty and a coquette.

The strangest thing of all was (so the people thought at least) that Kester's evil eye had no effect on Katie. She grew as strongly, and bloomed as hardily, as the wild briar in the hedgerow. Everybody remembered the five children who were born to him by his first wife; how they pined from their cradle. They had a sickly hectic in their faces like their mother; while Katie's cheeks were red as a damask rose: they crept about home weary and ailing always; while Katie was away in the woods, nutting and bird-nesting like a boy. Kester could deny her nothing, and she grew up, to the wonder of the village, healthier, more wilful, and bonnier than any girl in the district.

II.

THE blacksmith who had succeeded Kester Pateman at the village forge was a young man of
herculean strength, and a wild character. He
was more than suspected of a tenderness for the
Squire's pheasants, but the gamekeeper had not
yet been found bold enough to give him a night
encounter in the woods; his name was Rob
Mc'Lean; he had been a soldier, and was dis-
charged with a good-conduct pension, after ten
years' service, and two wounds. He was Katie's
first sweetheart. She was very proud to be seen
walking with him in the green lane on Sunday
nights; but it was more child's pride than anything else, for when he began to talk about
marrying, she laughed and said no, she was not
for him, he was too old.

Jasper Linfoot, the miller's eldest son, next
cast his eyes upon her, and followed her like
her shadow for a month; but no—Katie did not
fancy him, he was too ugly: he squinted, he had
red hair, and his legs were not both of the same

length. Then there was Peter Askew, the
squire's huntsman, but he was a widower; and
Phil Cressy, the gardener, but he was a goose;
and Tom Carter—but Katie could never abide
a tailor.

While Katie, very hard to please, was co-
quetting with her would-be lovers, perfectly safe
and perfectly heart-free, Kester Pateman had
settled all the time whom she should marry—
Johnny Martin, and nobody else. Johnny was
the only son of Martin, the Squire's coachman,
who had saved money. He was a simple young
man, with lank hair, a meek expression of countenance, and some gift for expounding, which he
practised to small select congregations in Pateman's barn every Sunday evening. When Kester
announced his intention to his daughter, Katie
pouted her red lips and tossed her head, saying,
with an accent of superlative contempt, "That
Johnny!" But she answered neither yea nor
nay to her father's words; and the next Sunday
"that Johnny" came courting, with a little basket
of cabbages on his arm, as an offering to his
belle.

Katie looked as if it would have done her heart good to fling them one after the other in his fat, foolish face, but she restrained the impulse, and only said,—

" I'll plant 'em out to-morrow, Johnny."

" Plant them out, Katie! Why, they're to eat."

" Pigs?" asked Katie, in innocent bewilderment. " We don't keep any."

" No, they're for you, Katie; they're the finest white-hearts."

" Hearts! Oh, Johnny, take 'em away directly; hearts!—I never saw a heart before," and she peeped into the basket with a face of horrified curiosity.

Now, Johnny had proclaimed that his affections had fallen on Katie because she was such a clever girl, and could do everything; but this exhibition of her talents by no means equalled his former impressions. He tried her again—

" Can't you cook, Katie? Did you never stuff and roast a heart for your father's dinner?"

" Oh, Johnny, and you putting up for the schoolmaster's place; what wicked nonsense you are talking! Surely you've called at the Blue Cow by the way?"

Johnny at this monstrous insinuation broke out into a cold perspiration; he was the most abstemious of young men, and had a name in the village for every variety of excellence; and Katie was quite capable of telling her suspicions everywhere. He endeavoured to take her hand and to put his arm round her waist; but Katie brought her palm against his cheek with such hearty good-will, that he was fain to subside upon his chair in meek dismay.

"If you do that again, Johnny Martin, I'll tell my father," she cried; and, with an affectation of great anger, she bowled his cabbages out into the garden, and ordered him to march after them in double quick time. He took up his hat and obeyed her, casting on her, as he went, the most pitiful and expostulatory glances.

"Don't stop at the Blue Cow, Johnny; go straight home," she cried, as he went out at the gate, and the defeated swain crept away quite dejected.

Katie returned into the house, and began to

sleek her hair before the little glass by the kitchen
fire, humming a tune all the time, and thinking
how well she was rid of Johnny, when that
worthy's voice sounded through the open window,—

"I didn't stop at the Blue Cow, Katie." She
turned smartly round, with such a shrewish face,
that Johnny added, in haste to deprecate her
wrath, "I left my basket, Katie; let me get
it—it's in the corner."

"At your peril, set foot over the door-stone,
Johnny!"

Johnny's plump countenance instantly disappeared. She snatched up the basket, threw it
after him, and then took a hearty fit of laughter
to herself.

III.

It was the beginning of harvest; and, on the
evening of the day after Johnny Martin's inau-
spicious courting visit, Kester Pateman and Katie
were sitting on the wooden bench before the door,
she knitting, and he bemoaning, when a party

of Irish reapers, with their sickles in their hands, came up the lane. They stopped at the gate, and one of the men asked if Kester wanted hands for his corn?

"No, I see nae the use o' hands," replied the old man; "it'll all be spoilt."

It had been a splendid season, and Kester's little fields showed as rich and ripe a crop as any in the country; it was quite ready for cutting, and the weather was settled and favourable.

"But, father, you must have hands," said Katie, who had a most irreverent disbelief in the evil eye; "two reapers and a binder, with you and me, will get the crops in this week, and I'll overlook 'em for luck."

Kester stopped two men and a lad, and bade the others go higher up the lane to Marshall's farm.

"But where's the good of it, Katie?" he added. "You'd have had a tidy fortune, but for me. Go into the barn, lads, you'll get your supper 'enow."

The old man was very despondent; for he

had just lost a fine calf, which he thought to
sell at a good price. Katie bade him cheer up,
and went indoors to set out the supper for the
reapers. When it was ready, she called to them
to come, and three as Ragged Robins as ever
might have served for scarecrows appeared at
her bidding.

One of them was a tall, fine young man, with
a head well set upon his shoulders, a roguish
eye, and a very decided national tongue. He
looked at Katie, and she at him; and, for the
first time in her life, the girl's eyes fell, and her
colour rose. Alick seemed slightly bashful too
—very slightly—for, after dropping his glance
on his plate for a second, it followed Katie to
and fro in the kitchen without intermission, until
she went out into the garden again. Alick could
see her through the branches of briar across the
window, standing at the gate with her father, talking to Rob Mc'Lean, and he immediately conceived
an intense dislike for that well-built son of Vulcan,
with the scar across his forehead. Alick jumped
to conclusions very quickly; he had fallen in
love at first sight, and was ready to quarrel

with any man who so much as looked at Katie.

Having made an end of his supper, he went out into the lane to his comrades, who were sitting under the hedge resting, and munching lumps of bread and cheese—Marshall's kitchen not being big enough to hold them all. Alick kept Katie at the gate in sight; and, though she seemed never to look his way, she knew perfectly well how he watched her; and, moved perhaps by the natural spirit of coquetry, she marched with her knitting into the house, and shut herself up in her bedroom. It had a window looking on the lane, and Katie sat near it with her pins and stocking, peeping out sometimes to see how the evening went on, and whether there was promise of fine weather next day to cut the corn. Alick wandered off by-and-by. How should he know that tiny lattice in the, bushy pear-tree was Katie's?

IV.

ALICK, Kester, Katie, and the rest, were all in the fields next morning as soon as the sun was up. The reaping began. Katie would bind for Alick; and, during the day, the two exchanged a good many sharp words. Rob Mc'Lean came to lend a hand in the afternoon, and the men soon found each other out; but Rob had a decided advantage over the other.

" Was there ever such a wild Irishman, all tatters and rags, seen in the country-side before ?" whispered Rob to Katie, as they sat under a tree, at four o'clock, eating the 'lowance that had been brought from the house.

Katie gave Alick a sly glance, and said, " No." And as Alick overheard both question and answer, he vowed vengeance against Rob.

That night in the lane there was Jasper Linfoot and Phil Cressy; and Katie talked and laughed with both of them; and the next day she was gossiping with Peter Askew, over the field-style; and in the evening Tom Carter

brought her some shreds of scarlet cloth that
she wanted to weave into a mat, and Katie
chattered with him; and the next day Johnny
Martin came, with an offering of summer apples,
which (Alick being there to see) were graciously
accepted. So Johnny was heartened into staying
half an hour, sighing and smiling spasmodically.
Alick went out very wrathful. "So many rivals
are too many for one man," thought he. And
all the following morning, he took no more notice
of Katie than he did of Kester—I mean, he
seemed not to take notice of her.

Katie was as cross as sticks, and pretended she
was ill, and must go home. Home, accordingly,
she went, and tangled her knitting horribly. She
had not been there long, when Alick came in
at the gate, with a long face, holding his hand
in a handkerchief all stained with blood. Up
sprang Katie, the colour going out of her face
with fright.

"You're hurt, Alick! Oh, how have you done
it? Let me see and bind it up."

"The least bit in creation, Miss Katie; but
you're the best binder in the world, and it'll heal

under your eyes," replied the wily Alick, un-
covering the injured hand.

Katie got a sponge and water, and bathed it,
and her pity fled.

"It's not much more than a scratch," said she;
so Alick groaned miserably.

"Surely, Miss Katie, it's the hard heart you've
got, for all your bonnie face," said he, reproach-
fully.

Katie blushed. Nobody else's compliments had
ever had that pleasing effect before; and Alick
suddenly took heart of grace, and said one or
two more pretty things that did not seem to vex
Katie very much. The dressing of the wound
being done, Alick was obliged to go back to the
field; carrying the 'lowance was an excuse for
Katie to return too; so, leaving her ball to the
mercy of the cat on the floor, she got the basket
and stone bottle of beer ready, and followed Alick.
The reapers said 'lowance was early that day, and
her father found fault about it.

Alick's reflections were of a more cheerful turn
now.

"Too many rivals may be as good as none,"

he thought. Indeed, he had found out—who
knows by what freemasonry?—that Katie liked
nobody as well as him; and he turned his discovery to good account. Did she encourage Rob,
or Jasper, or Peter, or Johnny, or any one of
her many admirers, by word or smile, he devoted
himself to Jennie, the pretty Irish girl, who was
binding at Marshall's farm; and Katie's pillow
could have testified that he had ample revenge.

Thus they went on till the last shock was
in stack, and the Irish reapers began to travel
north in search of fresh pastures. All went
but Alick; and he, from his quick wit and
sharp eye, had won favour with the Squire's
head keeper, who retained him as one of his
watchers.

Although he had arrived at Harwood a scare-
crow of rags, who so trim and spruce now as
Alick? Katie had a secret pride in his appearance, as, with his gun on his arm, and his game-
bag slung over his shoulder, he followed the
Squire in the woods—looking, as she thought,
far the finer and handsomer gentleman. "That
Johnny's" face had now become perfectly sicken-

ing to her, and none the less so because Kester
would talk of their marriage ; for the young man
had been chosen village schoolmaster, with a
salary of thirty pounds, a cottage and garden rent-
free, and coals ad libitum ; so that he had a home
to take her to.

Katie was having a good cry one afternoon, in
the house by herself, over the thoughts of Johnny,
when there came a knock to the door. She got
up and opened it, expecting to see a neighbour
come in for a gossip ; but, instead, there stood
Alick.

Directly he saw what she had been about he
cried,—

" Who has been vexing thee, Katie ? Only tell
me—tell me, Katie ! "

And a smile broke through her tears as she
said,—

" Oh, Alick, it's that Johnny ! " And they
looked in each other's faces and laughed.

What Alick said more, this tradition betrayeth
not ; but, whatever it was, Johnny's prospects of
a wife were not increased thereby ; and when
Alick went away home to his cottage at the park

gate, it was with a triumphant step, and his
curly head in the air; and Katie cried no more
over her knitting that afternoon.

V.

VILLAGE gossip soon proclaimed the fact of
Alick's visits to Kester Pateman's cottage; and
amongst the first to hear of them was Johnny.
He went and remonstrated with Katie, and
threatened to tell her father. Katie's blood was
up, and she dared him to tell at once. So Johnny
did tell, and Kester bade Alick keep away.

"Katie's for no Irish beggar, but for a decent
Harwood lad," said he, surlily. "And you'll
come about my place no more, Sir Gamekeeper,—
d'ye hear?"

Alick feigned obedience; but he and Katie
met in the green lane on Sundays. There was
a little gate from the pasture where Kester's
cows were, into the wood; and often, at milking
time, you might have seen Alick leaning over
the gate, talking to Katie at her task; but, as
the evenings grew cold and the cattle were

brought up to the house, these meetings were less frequent; for Kester began to watch his daughter as a cat watches a mouse. He suspected her.

The neighbours noticed Katie had become graver and paler, and shook their heads portentously. "She's fading, like the rest of them," they said; "she'll not see the spring. Kester's smitten her, poor man!"

And, by-and-by, Kester saw the change himself. When he did see it, his heart stopped beating. "Why, Katie, my bairn!" cried he, with fully awakened love and fear; "Katie, my bairn! thou's not going off in a waste, like thy brothers and sisters?"

Katie was knitting by the firelight; and, as her needle went, her tears fell. "I don't know, father; but the neighbours say I look like it. I'm sick and ill——" And her tears flowed faster.

Kester kissed her, and went out in a black mood.

"Oh, what'll I do? What'll I do for thee, Katie, my bairn?" said he, aloud. "I'm fit to tear my eyes out o' my head! What have I done, that all goes ill with me?"

It happened that Alick was loitering about in the hope of a chance word with Katie, and he overheard Kester's lamentation.

"What's the matter, Master Pateman? Katie's not ill, is she?" he ventured to ask.

Glad to unfold his misery to anybody, Kester told Alick of his daughter's changed looks, and what everybody attributed them to.

"Go to the wise man, 'Bram Rex, at Swinford, to-morrow: he's got a charm agen the Evil Eye," suggested Alick, in haste. "He'll tell you what to do: you may trust him."

Somewhat comforted, Kester re-entered the house. Alick went off to Swinford to prepare the sage for his visitor the next day.

VI.

"WHERE are you going, father?" Katie asked, the following morning, as her father came to breakfast dressed as if for church or market.

"I'm going to 'Bram Rex, Katie, to hear what

he says about something.   He's a wonderful
wise man."

"Is it about the stacks, father?   I'd fear none:
all's right so far.   Them Irish reapers brought
you luck, I'm thinking."

"It's not about the corn, Katie,—but thee.
I maun't lose thee, my bairn.   Alick says
'Bram has a charm, and I'm going to get it for
thee.   I don't like thy white looks and thy
crying."

Katie dropped her spoon, and smiled to herself as she stooped to pick it up again, with a
face like a rose, which she was fain to hide by
looking away through the window for ever so
long.

After breakfast, Kester mounted his old grey
mare, and went slowly to Swinford, very mournful, and much troubled in his mind.   The village
of Swinford was, by the river, seven miles from
Harwood, and the high road ran along the bank,
with a steep fall to the water, which was covered
with hazel and low shrubs.   "Wherefore shouldn't
I fling myself in there, and save the poor bairn?"
he said to himself, as he saw the river shining

and glancing through the bushes. "But, after all," he added, " it will be as well to see old 'Bram Rex first, and hear what he's got to say to her. My poor bairn! poor Katie!"

So he went forward to a small slated cottage at the entrance of the village, and knocked at the door.

"Come in," said a rough voice. Kester fastened his bridle to the paling of the garden, and entered.

The wise man was sitting in a large chair by the fireside, stirring a composition in a pan which had far more of the perfume of a poached hare than hell-broth, which the gossips said he was in the habit of making. 'Bram was an old man with a long beard, and the subtlest and most wily of smiles. He looked up at his visitor from under his brows cunningly and shrewdly, then motioned him to be seated by a wave of his hand. Kester was not here for the first time; many a half-crown had he paid 'Bram for prognostics touching the weather, information about lost articles, and charms for his cattle against disease, and his crops against blight; but he had never before felt such a perfect submission to the awful sage in the chair covered with cat-skins.

"I know your errand, Kester Pateman," said 'Bram, solemnly. "I have been working out the horoscope all night. It is a case of difficulty."

Kester was profoundly impressed by this pre-science, and his poor old hands shook as he drew out his leathern purse, and said,—

"'Bram, it's not money nor corn this time, it's my bairn Katie."

The sage nodded and echoed,—

"Katie! I knew it."

"What must I give you? This?"

And Kester took out a gold piece, and laid it on the seemingly unconscious palm of 'Bram.

"Enough, Kester Pateman," replied he; "enough. Tell me what you want—your daughter is smitten——"

"Yes, 'Bram; but there was one told me you had a charm agen the Evil Eye. Would it save her? Will you sell it?" asked Kester, trembling all over with anxiety, and stretching out his feeble hands with the purse to 'Bram.

'Bram took the purse, but said, severely,—

"I do not sell, Kester Pateman—talk not of selling. Describe to me your child's symptoms, and be at peace."

The wise man had a voice of such preternatural depth that it really seemed as if his words were also of superior sagacity; Kester listened to him with the profoundest faith, and then gave a description of Katie's state—her pale cheeks, her stillness, and her crying. 'Bram shook his head.

"I don't say she'll die, Kester, and I can't say she'll live; but there's one chance, if you'll try it."

"I'll do anything, 'Bram—why, I'd die for that bairn! You don't know how I love my Katie. What's the chance, 'Bram?"

"The stars will not be hurried, Kester Pateman; they have not spoken yet. Come and see."

The sage led the way into a second room, in the middle of which was a table whereon lay a sheet of paper with sundry figures and scrawls thereon.

"Look here," and 'Bram began to trace a line with his forefinger. "This is the girl's line of life. Mark it well, Kester Pateman."

Kester, dizzy with anxiety, fixed his eyes on it intently.

"Here is a man of battles; it passes him. This part shows them that seek her in matrimony; them that she must not marry, Kester—you mark me?"

Kester nodded his head.

"She must not marry any one of these with the cross agen 'em. Not this with the spade, nor the figure with the sack, nor him with the tailor's goose, nor yet this man leading of a horse, nor yet that one with the peaked cap and ferule—the stars have spoken agen 'em all."

Kester wiped his forehead, and said he saw that clearly enough.

"Mark me agen, Kester," pursued the sage, sinking his voice until it sounded as if it came up out of the toes of his boots; "mark well, for I can't show you it a second time. This is the sign of a powerful man who has come over the sea— he's got a sickle and a gun. The sickle means that he shall reap abundance o' corn, and live on the fat o' the land all his days, and the gun is a token that he's a brave man; and his face being to Katie's line o' life is a sign that he loves her, and that she has a thought for him. Are you hearkening, Kester? "

" Yes, 'Bram, I hear. Oh! but you are a knowledgeable man. These," following the first marks with his fingers, " are surely Rob Mc'Lean, and Jasper Linfoot, and here's Phil Cressy, and Peter Askew, and Tom Carter, and Johnny Martin——"

" Them's their names! None o' 'em must your Katie marry, the stars has otherwise bespoke for 'em. Do you know who this last is, Kester? "

" It maun be Alick, the wild Irish reaper; him that's at the Squire's now."

" Him it is, and no other! The interpretation thereof is just!" said 'Bram, emphatically, and he rolled up the sheet of paper.

Kester Pateman was greatly in awe of 'Bram, but he endeavoured to protest against the conclusion.

"'Bram, couldn't you bring forward another?" said he, hesitatingly.

"Can I alter the stars, Kester?" replied the sage, in his sternest tone. "I do not make, or mend, or mar, I only read for the blind what is written. You must give your bairn Katie to Alick, or she'll die."

"Oh! I will—surely I will, 'Bram!" in great haste cried poor Kester. "He's honest if he's poor, and Katie'll not have a penny. Tell me, Kester, will I sell my corn well this time?"

"You shall," responded 'Bram; "you shall sell it as others do."

"Have you that charm agen the Evil Eye that one told me of, 'Bram?" Kester humbly inquired.

"Yes, Kester; but it is not to be bought with silver nor gold. Send me half a bushel of your best aits, and you shall have it. I've parted with a many, but I've only one on hand now, and it's a good one."

"Let me have it, 'Bram. You'll get the aits to-morn."

'Bram went to a drawer in the dresser, and, after rummaging for some minutes amongst its contents, he brought forth a hare's foot with a string attached to it. He smoothed it carefully with his hand, muttering a formula of words to himself as he did so.

" You must put this in your pillow, Kester, and every morning, the first thing when you get up, open the window, and fix on some particular tree or bush, and look at it steady while you spell your own name backwards three times. You must look every day fasting at the same thing, and in time it will wither away and die. And so you'll be cured, and in smiting the tree the rest o' your things 'll be safe."

Kester took the hare's foot as tenderly as if it had been a sacred relic, and put it in his bosom.

" Thank you, 'Bram—and you're sure Katie 'll be well if I let her wed Alick ? "

" Yes, man ! You'll find the lass's face shining when you get home, for she's feeling that your heart's changed towards her already. The stars has been whispering of it to her."

Quite cheerfully Kester trotted the grey mare home, and, as if immediately to prove the sage's words true, Katie came to meet him at the gate as

rosy as a peony. Alick, at that minute, was
escaping by the cow-house door into the pasture,
after telling Katie of his visit to 'Bram Rex, and
preparing her for its probable results.

VII.

In the centre of the great meadow directly opposite Kester Pateman's chamber window there was
a fine old oak-tree, quite in the maturity of its
years and strength. Under its wide-spreading
branches a herd of cattle could shelter from the
summer heat, and in its giant bole was timber
enough to build a frigate almost. When Kester
rose the morning after his visit to 'Bram Rex, he
opened his window, and his eyes fell on this tree
the first thing, as they had probably done for
many a year. This time he gazed at it fixedly,
half expecting to see the leaves and branches
shrivel under his gaze; but he spelt his name
backwards three times, and there were no visible
effects. He went to market after breakfast and
sold his corn, and bought a new cow; so implicit
was his faith in 'Bram's charm; and, meeting

Johnny Martin, told him ruefully, that he must leave off thinking of Katie; for she was not permitted to be his wife.

"Why not, Master Pateman?" demanded Johnny, to whom this sudden change was incomprehensible.

"Because thou's bespoken, Johnny, for another woman; and there'd be contradiction and the mischief and all if we tried to go agen what's ordained. I spoke to 'Bram Rex yesterday—it was he tell 't me."

"'Bram Rex! the vagabond fortune-teller!" exclaimed Johnny, puffing out his fat cheeks in token of contempt, for Johnny pretended to more light than his neighbours. "Is that Katie's best reason, Kester Pateman?"

"Maybe not, man; she's no inkling that I've changed my mind yet. I 'an't spoken to her, but I maun."

"But it's not fair to jilt a poor fellow, because 'Bram Rex tells you a pack of lies," remonstrated Johnny. "I'll speak to Katie myself, with your leave, Master Pateman, and ask her her reasons."

" Her reasons, Johnny, is that she can't abide thee; thou's a good lad, but it goes agen the grain with her to think o' thee. She's a saucy lassie, and her that's bespoken you by the stars has a mint of money."

This happy invention of Kester's was uttered boldly as a consolation to the forsaken swain, and he, as such, accepted it. Johnny was as credulous as his neighbours.

In about a month after Kester Pateman's visit to 'Bram Rex there was a wedding at Harwood, and such a dance in Kester's barn as had never been heard of in the country-side before. All the defeated swains were there. Johnny Martin and Tom Carter made the music on two independent-minded violins, and lost, in this opportunity of distinguishing themselves, the sore sensation of disappointment. Johnny behaved nobly; he presented Katie with half a peck of apples as a wedding present, and looked glorious all night. When Katie came near him once he whispered,—

"Katie, did you tell anybody about the Blue Cow ? "

"No, man; it was only my fun," replied she, mischievously; and Johnny drew a long breath of relief.

What a dance that was to the tune of "Merrily danced the Quaker's wife, and merrily danced the Quaker!" It seemed as if it would never come to an end. So loud and hilarious was the mirth at the supper after it, that nobody heard the thunder rattling overhead, or saw, when all separated and went home, the lightning leaping about the hills. But there had been certainly a terrible storm that night, though few people at Harwood recollect it; and the next morning, when Kester opened his window, as his custom was, to give the charmed gaze at the oak-tree in the meadow, behold! one side was reft entirely of its boughs, and a black scarred trunk faced him instead of yesterday's majestic growth. Kester started back affrighted. Could this be the effect of his Evil Eye?

If you ever go to Harwood, as you ride into the village, in the meadow opposite the black-smith's forge you will see the blasted trunk of the giant oak-tree; and, should curiosity prompt

you to ask how it came to be destroyed, any
gossip will tell you that one Kester Pateman
withered it away by the power of the Evil Eye—
he having gazed at it every morning, fasting,
for that purpose. They will tell you also that,
from having been one of the most unlucky of
men, he became one of the most prosperous in
the district, with grandchildren and great-grand-
children, and flocks and herds innumerable.

Alick and Katie still live in the farmhouse
down by the water-pasture, which the Squire
let them have when they were married. By
dint of talking of it, they have come themselves
to believe in the Evil Eye. 'Bram Rex's de-
scendants live and flourish in various districts;
though 'Bram himself, for some mistake respect-
ing another person's property, was transported
to a distant colony to exercise his craft there—
with what success, this tradition sayeth not.

From the Diary.

—⚬—

"AND that is the end of it," said Miss Mostyn, laying the manuscript aside.

"It will do," pronounced my pickle of a Belle. "There was *some* fun in you, mamie, when you were young, for all Hannah says you were so solemn. Do you think there is time for another story before papa comes home?"

"No, my dear," replied Miss Mostyn, seriously. "Our tea will have been carried into the schoolroom, and there are to-morrow's lessons to prepare."

I did not gainsay the governess, so Belle tied up the portfolio, shouldered it with some show of exertion, and informing me that she knew of a nice safe place to keep it in—namely, the old trash closet—she went away to her own domains.

My dear child is very outspoken, but I think her own warmth of heart will preserve her from blundering upon the tender feelings of her relations and friends, which is a danger some ready-tongued people often risk.

When Emmy and I were left to ourselves, we had a little quiet talk over the great event of the day, and then leaving James to clear away the dessert, and set the table for tea, we adjourned upstairs to dress against the return of Felix and Mr. Dover. Neither of us said so, but, of course, we expected Mr. Dover to come in to drink tea and spend the evening.

I was writing a little letter to Steenie, when I heard the phaeton drive round the avenue, so I waited upstairs until Felix came to me. He looked frosty-faced but cheerful, so I perceived, at once, that Mr. Dover's unbosoming had been agreeable to both.

" Well, Katie, where is she ? " asked he, having first ascertained by a glance round the room that Emmy was not hiding in any of its shady corners.

The next moment she came running in, and throwing her arms round his neck, kissed him and cried, "Oh! papa, papa!" It was all out of her happiness, but she could not help a rush of tears; so after a little sensible rallying and soothing, he left her to me, and in a short time we were enabled to appear quite smiling and rosy in the drawing-room, where the curate was standing on the hearth-rug, recklessly breaking up a whole spill-case of my cedar-wood matches and casting them into the fire. He recovered himself rapidly, and we shook hands;—from the first Mr. Dover has seen that I was his friend;— and then I suppose he gave Emmy his news from the clerical meeting, for they laid their heads together and had some very serious talk over the blotting folio in which the botanical specimens are dried.

Felix had not much to tell me. As usual, Mr. Close and Mr. Sharpe had been the chief speakers; and poor Mr. Travis had fallen asleep. The doctor says his circulation is so slow, that there is danger of his being attacked by paralysis of the brain; he would be a sad loss to

Bowerham, for I do not know anywhere a better man, or better parish priest.

And so this celebrated day came to an end.

This afternoon, just as it was beginning to darken, and Emmy and I were sitting over the dressing-room fire, holding a consultation about a matter of no great significance, Belle came in beguilingly with—"Oh! mamie, what a dull fire you have here! We have such a beauty in the schoolroom; I wish you would come—and I want to show you a drawing that I have finished to-day." I knew in a moment what the sly little pussy's invitation meant.

Emmy and I closed our business at once, and adjourned to Miss Mostyn's quarters, where we found set out all in form the portfolio of scraps, the green lamp, the old sofa so comfortably stuffed, and my idle-time knitting.

"It is going to be a Legend of a Haunted House this time," announced Belle, appointing our places. "A story about Eversley, where mamie was born. It will last us three or four days. Now, mamie dear, will you read the beginning?"

" No, Belle; it is quite sufficient that I wrote without being condemned to read it," said I, decisively, so, in the end, the manuscript was given over to Miss Mostyn again; and it could not have been in better hands, for she is a very expressive and touching reader indeed.

THE HAUNTED HOUSE.

I.

THE HOUSE IN NEVIL'S COURT.

In one of the courts in the vicinity of Eversley Minster, there lived many years ago an engraver, Nicholas Drew by name. He was a quiet, inoffensive old man, of retired habits, who minded his own business, and was charitable according to his means. He occupied the whole of the second floor of the house, to which he ascended, not by the common stair-way, but by a flight of rude wooden steps, which he had himself constructed beneath the centre window of the room where he worked at his craft.

The curious in such matters said that Nicholas Drew's etchings were unique; but the probability is, that they brought him small gain; for though

individuals were well inclined to turn over the
contents of his folios, they were less disposed to
pay the high prices which the old man set
upon his works. He lived alone, and seemingly
quite contented with his lot; but it was a
tantalizing mystery to the people of the court
how he used the six rooms he rented; and
though his appearance was that of meagre, nay,
of sordid poverty, the gossips presently concluded
that he possessed a fabulous amount of wealth,
hidden away in the locked chambers. Close on
this rumour followed another, which, a couple
of centuries before, would have consigned him
speedily to either stake or gibbet; but which
now drew on him nothing more terrible than the
ill-concealed dislike of his neighbours, and the
jeers of little children, who would have quivered
to their shoe-ties if he had but turned and scowled
at them.

It must be allowed that Nicholas did not carry
a good introduction in his face : it was a stern,
grim, unkindly countenance, not unlike the corbel-
heads by the gateway of the court. His sharp
grey eyes peered anxiously from beneath frown-

ing grizzled brows, a dishevelled beard lay outspread upon his breast, and lank rusty hair curled
down upon his collar; he had a restless, choleric
nostril; a high, full, bald forehead—the one commendable point of his physiognomy; a small,
nervous figure, and a rapid gait. When he went
abroad, his worn, patched clothing was always
concealed beneath a dusky tartan cloak. He
generally chose wet days or twilight for his excursions; and under the cloak was his portfolio,
with a corner sticking out before and behind.
His head was invariably covered with a wide-
flapped felt-hat, which served partially the purpose
of an umbrella, and hid all but the lower part
of his face with its patriarchal appendage. In
his right hand was gripped a stout stick, the very
sight of which was protection enough against the
little mocking urchins in the street, who, with
precocious bravado and pitiful cowardice, would
fling a stone after him when he was quite out
of reach, and almost out of sight. If not pressed
for time, poor Nicholas would sometimes watch
for the temporary absence of his small enemies,
that he might evade their attacks; for, if truth

must be told, there was a heart under the old tartan that shrank from this universal hatred, and not seldom a hot salt moisture under the pent-house brow also. Some respectable people, passing the old man in the street, would vouchsafe him a nod, which he eagerly returned; he would have been glad to speak to them, but the opportunity was not given him; so the poor engraver plodded on his silent and cheerless way, secretly marvelling what kept everybody aloof from him, whilst he longed more and more each day of his life for friends and companionship. The fact was, he was clever, poor, and needy — not a desirable acquaintance, in short.

One snowy New Year's Eve, Nicholas crept forth in the darkness, with his portfolio under his arm, to pay a visit to a printseller in the Barbican, who had half promised to buy an etching of the Chapter-House interior, which the engraver had just finished. The wind was very high, and the blinding snow-flakes drove full in

the old man's face as he turned his back on the
Minster, and went down into Friargate; but
less chilled than ordinary—perhaps because he
had escaped his tormentors—and glowing moreover with a hope of ultimate appreciation, he bore
it indifferently, and strode through the crisping
snow with quite a light foot and almost a light
heart.

It is an impossibility to crush the elasticity out
of some natures. Nine men out of every ten
would have collapsed utterly and miserably under
a tithe of the disappointments that Nicholas Drew
had borne cheerfully, supported by a very moderate daily portion of coarse bread, and the love
of his art.

It did not take the old man quite half an hour
to reach his destination; but the printseller's
shop was already closed. Nicholas knocked at
the door for some ten minutes in vain; but at
last a surly-voiced lad appeared, and said his
master had some guests, and would not be disturbed.

" Then I'll come to-morrow morning," suggested
the engraver.

"I don't think you need, for I heard master say he had changed his mind; your pictures are so dear," responded the youth; and with that he shut the door in the old man's face.

"Well, God is good," gasped poor Nicholas, turning off the step, after lingering a few seconds; "God is good. I *might* suspect that He had forgotten Nevil's Court; but I know He has not; His time has not come yet, that's all. I wonder when it will?"

A woman came up, and begged of him; he tried to evade her, but she followed him closely.

"Master, for the love of Heaven—for the love of the mother that bore you——"

Her voice was hoarse and feeble; he soon outwalked her; but the echo of her words, "for the love of the mother that bore you," pursued him like a wailing prayer. He turned back, and found her standing on the Barbican bridge, gazing down into the blackness.

"Come away; what are you thinking about?" he asked, harshly; for his voice was toned to match his grim face.

"I can't tell; drowning, maybe. It is an

easy death, they say," was the whispered re-
sponse.

"Nothing of the sort; it is dreadful. When
anything tells you that, shut your ears: it is
damnation to hearken."

"Nay, master, but that is hard; as well die
at once as die by inches. Who condemns me
to live, and gives me no means?"

"You must wait till your hour comes; it is,
maybe, deferred that you may repent. You are
not to lift the latch of life yourself, and steal
away from your sorrows like a thief."

"I am not a thief, master."

"No; you only thought of becoming a mur-
deress."

"It is easy to talk, master; but it is not easy
to pine day after day, and to slink about ashamed
and ragged in the streets at night; it is not
easy to see people eye one suspiciously, and get
out of one's way, as if they were afraid to file
their clothes with touching mine in passing,—
that's not easy, master."

"Why, the very children spit at me! Little
things that can hardly go alone raise a shrill cry

as soon as I come in sight. Don't think you
have got all the rough bits of life to yourself."
They had come to the corner of the market-place,
walking as they talked. "Don't go down Barbican again to-night, 'for the love of the mother
who bore you.'"

He put a shilling into her hand—the last he
had—and pattered away homewards, hearing her
earnest "God bless you, master!" echoed in the
swirl of every gust that came cuttingly through
the thick snow against his cheek, as he scurried
along. All the bells in the city were alive,
clanging and clattering in every direction. Nicholas fancied the noise made the night warmer;
but the fact was, that his keen edge of disappointment about the etching was blunted by that
little exercise of human charity, and the blessing
he had earned; his heart was warmer within.

The exhilarated feeling did not go down until
he came within scent of a provision-shop. Poor
old fellow! it is sad that genius, if it has not
wherewith to eat, must hunger like coarser clay.
Nicholas had indulged a mundane vision of supper
in going to the printer's, which was now out of

his reach completely: it is even possible that
his eyes were not quite clear as the savoury gust
waft against his nostrils, and reminded him of
his failure in the Barbican; but he clutched
his portfolio very tight, and crossed the street,
trying to forget the gnawing emptiness under the
tartan in a dream of future well-deserved reputation, some day to be his.

The wind and the snow and the bells together
had got up a famous whirl in the Minster Yard,
and came tearing down College Lane in a perfectly reckless way as Nicholas turned into it.
It was all he could do to hold fast the cloak and
folio, the stick and hat, as he crept under the
projecting houses up to Nevil's Court; and there,
having gained the partial shelter of the gateway,
he paused to ascertain that he really had not
lost any of his adjuncts, and to shake the snow
from his garments before climbing his staircase.
He had reared the portfolio in a niche, long
since despoiled of its tenant, and was quietly
taking off his cloak, when a sound close at his
heels made him jump aside almost as if he were
bitten. Could one of his little persecutors have

lain in wait for him in such weather?—Oh, the depths of juvenile malice!—yet it seemed scarcely possible. However, in his alarm, Nicholas darted across the court, and feeling his way up the steps, unlocked his window-door, and entered the room in all haste to escape from the shrill taunt and laugh which he so dreaded.

"It is too bad," said he aloud, dropping his hat and cloak on the floor, "it is too bad: I don't know what it means. I never hurt anybody in all my life that I know of. Poor old Nicholas! you're a sad, miserable, despised old pauper. No, you're not either; you're not sad, you're not miserable by any means, and don't say so, for it is not true; you know it is not, and it is wrong in you to mention it."

He always talked to himself as to a second person; if he had not done so, his tongue would have stiffened with disuse.

Breaking up the block of coal which he had left smouldering in the grate, the room was filled suddenly with a dancing radiance; Nicholas chafed his withered hands in the glow, and as the snow on his beard began to melt in the heat, he shook the white flakes off, and said, more cheerily,—

" Well, this is pleasant; I wonder if that poor soul in the Barbican has got to warm herself at a fire. What business have you to complain with such a shelter to come to—eh, Nicholas Drew? Now let us look at our work."

He strode across to shut the door, which he had left ajar, and then with a groan remembered that he had left the portfolio in the niche.

" What is to be done?—has that little mongrel gone to bed yet?"

He advanced his head outside to listen, and hearing nothing but the heavy sweep of the ladened wind, he cautiously descended and reached the gateway, grasped the case, and was returning, when a child's sobs startled him again.

"Why don't you go home to your mamie, little one?" he asked, with what gentleness he could, stooping over a dark bundle crouched against the wall. He got no answer, but a kind of hysteric cry, and the figure shrank away from him farther into the shadow. "You must not stop here all night; you may get frozen to death. Tell me where you live, and I'll carry you home."

He meant it; here was one of his foes in trouble, and his anger was quite gone. To this offer was returned a series of shrieking sobs, very pitiful to hear; but the child would not suffer itself to be removed.

"What must I do?" said Nicholas, almost as much distressed as the stray child at his feet. After a moment's consideration, he determined to knock at the door of a woman who was a shade less uncivil to him than the rest in the court, and to ask her advice. There was so much noise of talking within, and such a clangour of bells without, that it was some minutes before he could make himself heard. At length the door was opened, churlishly enough, by the woman of the place, who, directly she saw Nicholas, said: "Are you wanting a light again, Master Drew? other folk can keep their fires in, if they have to leave home for an hour or two."

" It is not a light I want ; but here is some poor body's child lying under the gateway, crying. Come and see if you know whose it is."

"Bless me! a bairn out at this time, and on
such a night: it is lost maybe." And snatching a
candle from the table, round which sat a party of
extremely merry guests, she scudded across the
court, unmindful of the snow falling on her best
cap. The little creature lifted up her face at the
sound of a woman's voice. "Heart alive, why it
is the forrin' wood-carver's bairn!" cried Mrs.
Parkes. "Job, come out here. What's come of
Louis Duclos, that Adie's left here?" The husband appeared at the summons, looking rather
hazy and incapable, and desiring to know what
it was all about; to which his spouse contemp-
tuously bade him go back to his chimney-corner
for a blind owlet that could not see an inch
beyond his nose; an order which he obeyed
with commendable alacrity.

"You've a good fire in your room, I see,
Master Drew; with your leave I'll carry Adie
up there. Come, my bonnie bairn, come to me;
I'll take care of you," said Mrs. Parkes, in a
coaxing motherly way, which had due influence
over the child; who now, sobbing violently,
allowed herself to be lifted from the ground and

taken to the engraver's room. Nicholas had dropped the portfolio in his excitement, and it was not likely he should recollect to pick it up now. He followed Mrs. Parkes with the extinguished candle, and plunging into the room after her, stirred up the blaze again till every knob of the carved mantel and every panel twinkled in the glow.

"Here's a New Year's gift for you, Master Drew! I doubt some mischance has befallen the bairn's father, for Louis is not the man to let her be straying about alone of nights," said Mrs. Parkes, rubbing the child's benumbed limbs with rough yet kindly hands."

"If anything has happened, I will keep the little lass myself," replied Nicholas.

"Hush now! she is quietened a bit; she'll speak enow. Adie, bairn, where's father? don't you know?"

The small eerie-looking creature turned a pair of great dark wistful eyes on her face, and said, with a shrill gasping cry, "Oh, he's dead! he's dead!" and fell weeping again as passionately as before.

It was useless to question the child any further then, for she was utterly incapable of answering; and after vainly endeavouring to elicit something further, Mrs. Parkes gave her some bread steeped in milk, which she ate with avidity, and then laid her to sleep on a rude settee, where she presently sank into an exhausted torpor.

"I wonder whether what Adie says can be true?" observed Mrs. Parkes, reflectively. "She is not like other bairns, you see; she has strange flights and fancies for one so young; yet she can't have fancied *that*. You stop by her, Master Drew, while I go and ask them below if they know where Louis has been working yesterday and to-day. He was at the Minster last week; I saw him go out this noon, and at tea-time Adie went off to meet him, as she always does; then our folks came in, and we hadn't opened the door after till you knocked. His place is all dark: see."

They were standing in the doorway; the wood-carver's room was on the ground-floor, in an angle of the court opposite. Mrs. Parkes now cautiously descended the steps; while Nicholas turned back into the room, wishing that the noisy bells would cease for once. He came and looked at the sleeping child very earnestly, making a silent vow to keep her and cherish her as his own, if what she had said should prove correct. It was a pretty mobile face on which he gazed, delicate in feature and dusk in complexion, as if the mellow warmth of a southern sun glowed through the tender skin. She was not like an English child at all; the ripe hue of her lips, the high arch of her brows, and the black gloss of her damp loose hair, were all more or less indicative of foreign blood.

After the lapse of a quarter of an hour, or rather more, Mrs. Parkes returned, accompanied by an elderly man, whom Nicholas recognized as a foreigner, and the frequent companion of Louis Duclos. " The bairn was right; he is dead; mashed a-pieces almost," whispered the woman, looking with pitying awe at the little orphan.

" How was it ? " asked the engraver, working his fingers nervously, and moving nearer to the settee on which Adic lay, as if to protect her.

" He was working at a house in the Barbican,

and fell off a scaffolding; they took him to the
hospital with the bairn following; but before they
could get him there he died, poor fellow! When
Adie heard them say so, she took off like mad:
you may think them that was with him would be
so hurried they'd scarce heed her, expecting she
would come to some of us where he lived. She
meant to get in home all to herself, I fancy, and
couldn't, for she'd lost the key. Mr. St. Barbe
found it as he came to see after her, lying a few
steps down College Lane, under the houses where
the snow hadn't drifted: she must have dropped
it. You'll take it, Master Drew."

Nicholas took the key, and begged Mrs. Parkes
and St. Barbe to be seated. The Frenchman
politely and gravely complied; but the good
woman excused herself, saying that Job was growing cross at her staying away so long; and as he
was not in a state to hear reason, she must go,
but would come early in the morning to attend to
Adie's wants.

The two men being left alone together with the
unconscious child, exchanged first a few mutually
puzzling compliments, and then sat silent; for

St. Barbe had little English, and Nicholas no
French. At last the engraver, with exquisite
simplicity, thought he should simplify their difficulty by speaking his own tongue almost unintelligibly—as the Frenchman spoke it, indeed.
He began: "Sare, I wish keep Adie." St. Barbe
nodded two or three times emphatically. "I be
father to her, friend, everyting," added Nicholas,
raising his voice, extending his arms, and em-
bracing the air. "What say you, sare?"

"Bien, good, ver well!" responded St. Barbe,
with a long series of gesticulatory movements
expressive of satisfaction.

The affair being thus arranged to meet the
views of both, the silence was resumed. Nicholas
fidgeted about on his chair, feeling that on this
night at least he ought to offer hospitality, to
drink success to the new year, and a peaceful
departure to the old. But what had he, poor
fellow, in the corner-cupboard that was his larder
but part of a brown loaf and a pitcher of water?
—not gala-fare certainly. All at once, while
considering how he should supply his lack of
good cheer, the Minster bells stopped, and the

clock struck midnight. The two men shook
hands immediately, and wished each other many
good wishes; the Frenchman diffused himself
into a long compliment relating to Nicholas's
evangelic charity and title to prompt canoniza-
tion, which would have rejoiced the old engraver's
heart if he could have understood it. He then
said he must return to his wife and children,
who waited him with a little gathering of friends;
but before departing, he looked at Adie for a
minute, touched her little hand with his gray
moustache, murmured over her a few words,
which Nicholas thought sounded like a benedic-
tion, and finally bowed himself backwards out
of the room, almost losing his balance at the top
of the steps by feeling for a handrail that did
not exist. Nicholas shut the door after him, and
replenished the sinking fire; he then drew near
to Adie, and exulted over his New Year's gift,
forgetting at the moment how he had come
by it.

"What a wee birdie it is; what a tender wee
nestling!" said he, softly. He could scarcely
forbear snatching her up, and pressing her to

his beating heart, there and then; he would have done it but for fear of waking her. He said a great many things besides, very affectionate and very touching, from that stern, disappointed heart of his, before he could leave her to sleep un-watched; and when drowsiness at last overcame him, it was with the greatest reluctance he crept to his bed. More than once before the frosty January dawn broke on the window-panes, he came rustling to the settee in his tartan cloak, like a comic ghost with a beard, driven about by anxiety of mind. At each visit he lingered a few minutes, and then scudded back with wonderful agility, lest she should awake, and, seeing him, should be frightened.

Poor old Nicholas Drew's heart was singing a new song the whole of that livelong night, though he went supperless to bed.

II.

THE NEW CARE AND NEW PLEASURE.

WITH daylight came Mrs. Parkes, carrying Nicholas's portfolio, all drenched with melted snow.

" There, Master Drew, thank me for that," cried she, throwing it down on the table; " the bairns were just going to rive it open when I stopped 'em. Maybe the things inside will be no worse."

" Oh dear, oh dear, they are all spoiled ; what a pity !" groaned the old man.

He looked at the case dismally for a few minutes; then brightened suddenly as he turned to the fire, by which sat Adie, in a huge leather chair, with her tiny feet on a block of wood, and a basin of milk in her lap.

" Well, I declare," exclaimed Mrs. Parkes, in great bewilderment; " you are good friends already, I see !"

" Yes, we are," responded Nicholas, cheerfully.

"I don't know how it came about, I'm sure: do you, Adie?"

"I never called names after you, or threw stones," said the child, timidly.

"Bless its bonnie face, that it didn't!" gasped Mrs. Parkes, melting. "You are a good bairn, Adie; you'll never be rude to Master Drew, will you?"

"Father said it was cruel, and I must not. Oh, father, come back, do come back!"

She would have flung herself to the ground in a wild paroxysm of crying, had not the woman caught her, and, gently rocking her in her arms, succeeded in soothing her again.

"There, there, hush, my bairn, be quiet!" said she; and then added: "Now, Master Drew, I'll stay with Adie, if you'll go and see Mr. St. Barbe about the funeral. Let it be decent, though maybe poor Louis has left nothing. And buy a bit of black stuff to make her a frock: I'll sew it."

Nicholas went to the great press, and took thence a little bag; this was a pretence, for he remembered ruefully that it contained only a few copper coins: he was quite puzzled how to meet this sudden demand on his scant resources. He stayed pottering so long, that Mrs. Parkes, who shared the popular faith in his hidden wealth, began to think hardly of him, and to say to herself that he was but a grudging churl after all. She soon hit on an expedient for hastening him, and at the same time rebuking him for his supposed covetousness.

"Master Drew," said she, significantly, "I'd advise you to sell them black pictures of yours for as many shillings as you've asked pounds; then folks will buy them, for they're real beautiful, and you'll have something to give this bairn more than you seem to have got now."

Nicholas grasped at the suggestion eagerly; the value of his works would be the same whatever he took for them.

"They'll be too common if I sell them cheap to the printers; but I'll carry a set, the whole cathedral set, to Canon Paget," cried he; "and I'll take whatever he'll give."

"Just as you like, master; only recollect this growing bairn can't live as you've done; and if you keep her at all, you must keep her well. As for your pictures being common if they cost little, the commoner a good thing is the better, I should say. I'd as lief, and liefer, please a hundred poor men's eyes as one rich man's; maybe you don't think in that way."

This view of the matter had never presented itself to the engraver; he thought it worth considering, and wondered how it had missed him before. Coveting fame, he had lost the way to it by toiling exclusively for one order of minds. Are not the suffrages of the multitude as worthy—appreciation by the many who *feel* as worthy — as appreciation by the few who *judge?*

The snow still continued to fall: it was drifted up into great white billows against the buttresses at the north side of the Minster, and lay thick on every ledge, and arch, and moulding, bringing out the hoary darkness of the stone in strong relief. Nicholas had no eyes for it on this morning, as he tramped through the yet untrodden covering of the gardens, in his tartan and round hat. It was still too early for the children to be about, or it is greatly to be feared that his odd fluttering garments would have been made the mark of many a well-aimed snowball. He reached the canon's house unmolested, therefore, and gave a faint pull at the bell. After the lapse of a few minutes a florid butler looked out of a side-window, and, seeing who stood there, asked sharply what Nicholas wanted; and being told that he wished to speak to Canon Paget, replied that that gentleman was out of town, and would not return for a week. This was a totally unlooked-for disappointment; for some minutes after the red face had disappeared from the window, Nicholas remained standing under the portico, considering with himself what he should do next.

"I'll go down into the Barbican," he said at length, slowly descending the steps. "Yes, I will; Marsh has wanted these etchings a long while; he won't give much, but then I must have *something*. What does it matter to me whether they hang in his parlour or lie shut up in Canon Paget's folio? Nicholas Drew, you have been a fastidious, proud old fool. This little nestling that has fallen on your door-stone must teach you to mend your ways; it is high time you did, I'm sure."

Exhorting himself inwardly, the old man turned down College Lane into Friargate; and, avoiding the temptation to run in and see that Adie had not evaporated, or changed into anything of a less satisfactory nature, he went direct to the shop in the Barbican which he had visited the night before. Marsh was there, scolding his apprentice, and in a state of post-vinous excitement. He burst into a coarse laugh as poor Drew appeared, and came forward to the counter.

"Are you so sharp set as this, Master Nicholas?" cried he. "Bless you, man, I can't give your price for the plate, and I won't. Who is to buy it if I do, eh?"

"I have not come about that now; I have brought a set of the Minster etchings,—there are fifteen," replied the engraver, calmly. "You have coveted them often, Marsh, when I was not disposed to sell; what will you give me for them now?"

"What I've offered ten times before—half-a-crown a piece," replied the printseller.

"Make it two guineas," said Nicholas.

Marsh smiled with a rather surprised air; and well he might, for the engraver's previous demand was five guineas.

"We won't split for a matter of a few shillings; the thing's done," he answered; and then counted the money out on the counter at once, lest Nicholas should repent of his hasty bargain. Unrolling the etchings, he continued to eye them for some minutes with a genuine appreciation of their merits, and then said with unction:—

"I'll say this for you, Nicholas Drew, these etchings will fetch money when you and I are underground; there is not such a hand as yours in Europe at a Gothic building. It isn't only the form, and shape, and richness, you catch, or the light and shadow either; but it is the very spirit of the place, and your own genius you put into your pictures. You might have been the original designer of the old Minster; the love of it seems bred into your bones."

"It is, it is. Haven't I lived in the shadow of it from a lad?" cried Nicholas, warmed by Marsh's words into betraying his enthusiasm.

"Ay, that's it. Habit will tell. Come in, and have a glass this cold morning," suggested the printseller.

Nicholas excused himself, and started homewards. When half-way there, he remembered what he had been bade to do; and turning into a shop, he purchased some black stuff and a little hood for Adie; then, with the parcel under his arm, stopped at St. Barbe's.

The Frenchman was a clockmaker, living near the Minster gates. Being busy when Nicholas entered, he had not time to talk; but he gave him to understand in few words that he would not be interfered with in any arrangements that he might wish to make for either father or child. St. Barbe washed his hands of it entirely; good Master Drew was a man of evangelic kindness; he would leave all to him—all. He was a poor man himself, and could not be charged with any but his own household; he had hard work to support them often, and more to the same effect.

This was conclusive.

"I shall not trouble him again; the child is mine," said Nicholas, audibly, as he tramped away to the hospital, to make final arrangements for the funeral of the poor wood-carver. He had not done so much business for years as he did that morning; all Friargate was astonished to see the tartan in action so early, and marvelled greatly what could have excited him to such unusual exertions.

When he reached Nevil's Court, the children were all out making a snow-man; at the sight of them the old engraver felt quite a cold thrill run through his veins. He had forgotten them, in his excitement, until he came suddenly on the rosy shouting troop.

"Here's old Nick; let's pelt him; let's pelt him!" screamed an audacious urchin at the top of his voice. Half-a-score shrill youthful pipes took up the cry, "Old Nick, old Nick; pelt him; pelt him!" when, lo, with a burst, out came Job Parkes armed with a horsewhip! He

charged in amongst the youthful fry, overturn-
ing some, and administering a salutary lash to
others, until he had changed their tune into a most
dolorous minor. Job had received his orders
from his wife, and had been lying in wait to
execute them ever since poor Drew went out.
That was the last time he had to shrink from
the mocking youngsters; they did not soon forget their lesson.

III.

THE FLOWER OF NEVIL'S COURT.

By the time that spring came round again,
Nicholas Drew and Adie were quite settled and
at home together. The child had the run of all
the six rooms, and one especially was given up
to her. Here she had flowers which bloomed
splendidly in the wide sunny window, and a
pair of most musical linnets in a cage. She
was a stirring vivacious child, subject to wild
fits of laughter and rarer moments of gloom,
which gave Nicholas, who loved her as the very

apple of his eye, a strange uneasiness at times.
She was wayward and wilful also, but very
affectionate; not slow to offend, but prompt to,
seek forgiveness. She had no application, and
no striking or prominent talent. It was long
before Nicholas could coax her into learning to
read, although she was nearly eight years old;
she was, in fact, a little indolent, freakish,
loving thing, whose tears would gush at a sharp
word, and whose smiles were the essence of
heart sunshine; it took so little to make her
happy, that it grieved the old man to see her
otherwise, and the restraining hand he kept upon
her will was very light.

Though living in Nevil's Court, amongst poor
artisans and the like, Nicholas Drew was not
of their class; he had been born in that house
before it was let off in apartments, when his
father—a more flourishing individual than himself—had rented the whole of it. Few people,
if any, remembered this, though they felt that
he was not one of them; that his genius, his
education, and a certain innate refinement spring-
ing from a pure and gentle heart, made a wide

gulf between them, which not even the miserable old tartan or his visible privations could by any means bridge over.

Circumstances began to improve with him now for very natural reasons; he sold his etchings at a moderate price, and also condescended to give lessons in drawing at several schools in Eversley, which he had formerly refused to do; but he still adhered faithfully to the ancient cloak and the felt hat, while he delighted to see Adie dressed like a spring flower. It was quite a picture to watch them sitting side by side at the Minster; she with such a soft pomegranate blush on her face, and he as faded, grey, and antique in shape as the queer effigies niched above them. They also often walked in the streets together, and Adie's beauty was a far greater protection to him from gibe and sneer than ever his own scowl had been.

As she grew up, her disposition became quieter and more pliant, and she submitted to be sent to one of those schools which Nicholas attended. Here much was done towards disciplining her impetuous character, though her natural abhorrence of rules sometimes came out very strongly. She appeared ignorant in comparison with other girls, but she was not really so; for the good old engraver had taught her much biblical history from his stores of engravings, and imbued her with some desultory knowledge by relating to her pleasing or terrible narratives from general history. Her strongest instincts were in her affections; she did not judge, she *felt*; the reflective element seemed to have been omitted from her composition altogether. She never readily attached herself to her schoolfellows, and cared for nobody's companionship so much as Nicholas's. Him she regarded with an enthusiastic, devoted, childish reliance; he was at once the best, the wisest, the dearest, and the most picturesque of old men; she took pride in the tartan and the beard which others ridiculed, and identified herself so completely in all his ways and oddities, that it was not safe to allude to them before her.

"He is not like other people!" she echoed one day after a weak girl who had laughed at him,—"not like other people! No; how should

he be like them? Could he simper as men do
who have nothing in their heads but wind? He
has a great heart; he has a full brain. He could
have built the Minster, I tell you. He ought
to have lived long ago, and then he would have
been a master of that grand society of Francs
Maçons we read about to-day. He is a great
good man, and everybody else is—Bah! why
do you vex me? If you want to laugh, laugh
at some one I don't love." Adie had a dangerous light in her southern eyes, when she was
angry, that intimated very excitable passions,
and even the possibility of a quick blow following the hasty word. It was wise to refrain
from irritating her; her school companions acknowledged it with a dim confused fear and
admiration for the fervour and earnestness of a
temper so unlike their Saxon calm. Her gratitude, that was almost a passion; her imagination,
so vivid and so picturesque; her warm sunny
loveliness; attracted others even while they remained as a bar of separation between them.
She, as well as Nicholas, was not like other
people; but there was that about her which

made little spites and jealousies impossible; she
was beloved by everybody who knew her, and
Mrs. Parkes, to whom she was warmly attached
by the memory of past kindness, called her
alternately "poor Adie" and "the Flower of
Nevil's Court."

IV.

THE WILD WHITE ROSE.

ONE bright July morning,—it was Adie's birthday, and she was seventeen years old,—Nicholas
Drew was hard at work on a new plate of "St.
Servin's Abbey," a ruin near the river, while
the young girl was chirping a little French song,
when a stranger appeared in the court below, and
was heard to ask if Drew, the engraver, lived
there. One of the children pointed to the stairs,
and the individual ascended and came in. Nicholas took off his spectacles, and pushed a chair over
to the visitor, whom he supposed to be one of
those curious persons who were in the habit of
coming to see his pictures, and of going away

without purchasing any. His action was not very courteous, for he begrudged sorely the time taken from his work. The young man quickly undeceived him, however, by stating that he was himself an engraver on wood, and that he wished to learn the art of etching on copper from Nicholas, of whose skill he had heard in London, through a dealer in prints who possessed some of his works. Flattered and gratified that a pupil from so great a distance had been attracted to Eversley by the reputation of his genius, the old man gave him a cordial welcome, and promised to render him the instruction he required.

They sat conversing together a long time about their art, and Adie, with a bit of work for appearance sake, drew near to listen. The stranger—Laurence Royston was his name—had taken a seat with his back to the doorway, and though apparently quite intent on all Nicholas said, he still had time to steal many glances at the bright face by the old man's shoulder. At first sight Royston's countenance struck you as handsome; at the second, it pleased less; and at the third, its cold flickering eye and sinister mouth were the most prominent traits. His features were clear but sharp; his forehead high, bony, and pale, with tawny hair—golden, as the sun shone through it where he sat—waving loosely above it. His figure was tall, but slenderly built, and clad in a long olive coat with much embroidery on the seams and flaps. In his left hand, the fingers of which opened and contracted with a nervous movement, he held a wild white rose—gathered, perhaps, at the roadside as he came to the town, for he said that his lodging was at Crossley, a village two miles off; his right hand he kept buried in the breast of his waistcoat. But his voice was the most peculiar thing about him,—a false voice it might be called ; for though clear and softly modulated as a flute, it did not seem to come direct from the well of his thoughts, but to make many subtle turns by the way, lest it should express too much.

Adie, moved by curiosity, tried more than once to get a fair look at the stranger's face, but she was always baffled by meeting his eye the moment she lifted hers from her needle ; being caught in the fact, she blushed, and he involuntarily smiled, at which she blushed the more, and finally got up and changed her seat for one by the farther window. Laurence Royston, as if to avoid the hot sunshine, immediately twisted his chair round, by which, without its appearing intentional, he still faced her, and thus checked her scrutiny. Adie seemed not to observe his movement; but he saw by the quivering of her lips, and the dancing radiance in her eyes, that she was laughing to herself; and, secretly annoyed at such mirth where he would rather have made a grave impression, he said to Nicholas, " Your daughter is not used to so much solemn discourse, I think, Master Drew. She looks anything but well entertained."

The engraver lifted up his shrewd face, and glanced at Adie. "If you are tired of our talk, child, get away to your birds or your flowers," said he, gently. " I dare say it is often dull for her up here in Nevil's Court, sir ; but she pretends she likes it for my sake."

" I am not dull anywhere ; you ought to know I am not, Grizzie," retorted Adie, coming quickly behind the old man, and standing by him with her hand on his shoulder. "I am as happy as the summer day is long, and all through you. I was laughing just now at my own thoughts: my thoughts are strange sometimes; so strange, they make me laugh whether I would or no."

"This white rose for the fancy that made you smile by the window five minutes ago," cried Laurence Royston, offering the flower. Adie blushed and hesitated.

"What was it, child?" asked Nicholas; "some mischievous freak either planned or remembered?'

"Neither, Grizzie; it was—no, I cannot tell you what it was."

She glanced with some confusion at the stranger, and would have moved away, but Nicholas held her fast by the arm, and demanded what she meant by calling him "Grizzie" so irreverently before visitors. She gave him the gentlest possible pull by the beard, and ran off laughing saucily. The old man shook his head, and made a sort of half-apology for Adie's wildness, and then resumed his discourse anent his art, which Laurence Royston found infinitely less interesting than before. He could not help wondering where the girl was gone, and whether she would return before he went away. His eyes turned frequently to the inner door by which she had escaped, and he put off his departure from moment to moment until another hour had elapsed. He then rose to go in earnest; and while Nicholas and he were exchanging last words, the quick step and lilting voice of Adie made themselves heard. She came in, evidently expecting that the stranger had left; for she cried, " I've found it, Grizzie—found it after such a rummage ! " then stopped short, with a scarlet blush dyeing her face to its very brow. She carried in her two hands a large engraving outspread, at which Nicholas looked up in bewilderment.

" What is it, child ? Let me see," said he, curiously, while Laurence Royston stood by the door with a peculiar smile on his face, as if he experienced a vindictive pleasure in her confusion. With great and visible reluctance, Adie came forward to the table, and threw the picture upon it, glancing with a timid half-defiance at the stranger as she did so. Nicholas drew the engraving towards him: it was "Satan playing with Man for his Soul."

"Well, what does it mean?" asked the old man, much puzzled.

"Do you not perceive your daughter's drift, Master Drew?" said Royston, quietly, so quietly that Adie knew some sentiment was being strongly held in check. "She has a quick eye for a resemblance: she likens me in her mind to that unhappy man."

"Ah, I see it now," responded Nicholas, in a musing tone. "What expression in the face! He is meditating how he shall outwit his adversary and win the game, though it is going hard against him. Satan exults already; he *knows* the stake, once risked, is his."

They all three examined the picture for several minutes in silence. Its effect on each was different: Nicholas eyed it with critical appreciation of the genius which had infused such depth and mingling of expressions into the artist's work; Royston gazed at it with a look, first of cynical indifference, then of gravity, then of melancholy earnestness.

" It is a lost soul from the first move," said he, in a tone that caused Adie to lift her eyes from the picture to him,—" yes, little girl, a lost soul from the first move," he repeated, more gently. " There is no redeeming angel at the man's elbow; only two fiends grinning their triumph in their master's success. I don't see how the adversary is to be foiled; do you?"

The girl pondered a few seconds, and then made answer, with a certain regretful strain in her voice.

" No; good thoughts are all gone out of his mind. Fear and subtlety alone possess him; and the fear is greatest."

" Then you think good thoughts may have once lived in him?" asked Royston, gravely.

" Yes. No one is unmixed evil. Satan himself was a pure spirit once; he may have his lingering regrets—who knows?"

" He fell through ambition and pride, which are princely sins. What is this man's temptation?" pointing to the figure in the picture.

" The greed of gain, the meanest and basest of all," answered Adie, resting her finger on the piles of coin represented as heaped up before Satan.

Laurence Royston drew a deep breath, and was silent; Nicholas rolled the picture up, and pushed it from him.

"Take it away, Adie; take it away; we have had enough of it," said he. "It is an uncomfortable picture. What induced you to bring it out? There, carry it off, and put it carefully into the folio again."

The young girl obeyed, and when she returned to the room Royston was gone.

———

There was at this time living with Nicholas Drew and Adie a middle-aged woman who acted as a servant. She was called Martha, and was of a decent appearance, but moody countenance. Mrs. Parkes held her in especial disfavour, averring that Nicholas had picked her up in the streets: she was indeed the person he had met and relieved in the Barbican on the very night that Adie was taken into his house. It is needless to enter into her antecedents, to condemn her or to exculpate. Nothing of her history was known except to her master, and could only be guessed by her scrupulous avoidance of the pure young girl with whom she shared the charitable shelter of Nicholas Drew's roof. If possible, she would not meet her ; and if compelled to speak, what she had to say was couched in the fewest words. The engraver acquiesced in this reserve : his flower must not be sullied by one evil thought. Martha from her kitchen - window had seen Laurence Royston come and go. She had a singular habit of watching furtively, and garnering things up in her mind ; for what purpose it would be hard to say, as she never spoke of them afterwards ;—perhaps it was to mark their issues, and to feed her morbid craving for excitement by deducing remote possibilities from small beginnings. The first time she went into the room where her master and Adie were after Royston was gone, she examined the girl's face narrowly, and traced there a certain anxiety which was strange to its expression ; what did it portend ? While Martha was there, she began to sing again broken snatches of her merry songs, and throwing off the troubled thought, whatever it might be, resumed her natural easy gaiety. Martha thought she had caught the first slight thread of the web, and went away to brood upon it and wind laboriously through its meshes at her after-leisure.

She could not see yet whether it would be smooth or all pestered with knots and tangles, as so many are. She liked the girl, and wished her well for her master's sake, otherwise her saucy gaiety and instinctive pride would have jarred harshly with her own unstrung being.

When Laurence Royston descended the outside stairway into the court, he dropped the wild rose that he had carried in his hands upon the second step, where it lay unnoticed until after noon. Adie was standing at the window idle, when she saw it; for a minute or so, she looked at it through dreamy, listless eyes, then went out and picked it up. Martha observed the trivial action, and added another loop to the web. The poor little flower was soiled and crushed, its stalk broken, its leaves fallen, its scent almost gone.

"He threw it away," said Adie to herself, "and I think it is no better worth either." She whirled it from the window and it fell into the court below. "Now Grizzie would say that was wanton mischief," she went on, musingly; "he would not have anything of God's making treated with disrespect. That is a strange fancy of his, that the flowers feel, that they are susceptible of pleasure and pain. It may be so; they lift up their heads to the sunshine, they drink the dew, and grow, and bloom, and give forth sweet odours, their incense of prayer, their act of worship and thanksgiving; then they pine and die in unkindly frosts. If Grizzie be right, and I am inclined to think that he is, how that miserable little wild rose must feel its degradation, lying there in the dust to be trampled by any careless foot; this morning at dawn it was in some fresh green hedgerow, with hundreds of others that are blooming there still! I will go and rescue it."

Down she went, tripping noiselessly as a shadow, and, taking the sullied flower once more into her hand, but this time with a certain tenderness of gesture, returned with it to the engraver's room. Martha riveted a new knot on her thread. Nicholas was all the while diligently absorbed in his work, and he gave no heed to what was passing; besides, Adie was accustomed to utter her thoughts aloud without expecting any reply. She now came near him, and leant over his shoulder to watch him, as she often did; but, finding that he was too deeply occupied to notice her, she sauntered to her chamber where were her birds and plants. She spent some time chirping to the linnets, putting up her ripe red lips for them to peck at, and teasing them with the wild rose, which she struck gently against the bars of their cage. Wearying of such idleness at last, she breathed a little tired sigh, and looked at the broken flower.

" What am I to do with you now I have taken you out of the dust?" she said, as if she was speaking to a living thing. " You are too ugly to wear, too faded to put in a glass of water, for you will never revive again; lie there till you become unsightly as a weed, and then Martha will throw you away perhaps."

She laid it down by her looking-glass on the table before the window for that time; but at night, finding it still in the same place, she put it within a drawer amongst her few other treasures, where it stayed and was forgotten.

V.

THE OAK CLOSET.

In that large room where Nicholas Drew always worked there was a closet, lighted by a very small window that looked, not into Nevil's Court, but into an old-fashioned, luxuriant garden which lay behind the ancient bishop's palace. This closet was shut in by two elaborately carved doors of black oak, further ornamented by tarnished brass knobs. Adie had never seen more of the interior of this closet than that it contained a rude table and chair, and a cabinet of great antiquity; the window was darkened with a veil of smoke and dust as impervious to sunshine as the thickest curtain, and a general air of gloomy mystery pervaded the whole aspect of it. Nicholas rarely entered it; and when he did so, he remained shut up there for hours, and always came out saddened and depressed, as if he had been keeping a solemn vigil, or airing painful remembrances, or perhaps experiencing some renewed agony of remorse. Adie regarded it as a haunted place, and had no curiosity to spy into its secrets; not so Martha. She had a burning desire to know what was hidden behind those closed doors; for she did not give heed to the popular idea that Nicholas Drew was a miser, and kept his money in an iron chest. She believed rather that he laid his treasure up where it would accumulate at compound interest until his day of doom; and in that, doubtless, Martha was right. On the evening of the day of Laurence Royston's first visit, her master was shut up in the closet a couple of hours, while Adie, alone in the room, had much ado to keep herself out of mischief. Martha went in and out several times on various pretences; but Adie, who was singing by the doorway, and watching the children at play in the court below, paid no attention to her black gliding figure.

At last, towards sunset, the old man came out from his retreat, and would have resumed his

work, but the girl asked him to take a walk
with her. He acceded readily, and they went
together to the river-side. This was a favourite
resort for the town's-folk after the day's business
was over; for they soon escaped from the dust
and heat of the city into rural shades and sweet-
smelling meadows. There were consequently
many people abroad, enjoying the cool of the
evening and the pleasant sounds of country places.
Marsh, the printseller in the Barbican, with his
hat set very far back upon his head, met them,
and turned to have a chat with Nicholas. It
was not possible that Adie should be insensible
to the many eyes that looked and looked again
at the lovely face under her broad, coquettish
straw hat; it was a familiar face to most people
who took their pleasure at this time of day, but
custom stole nothing from its beauty. Marsh
himself, though generally chary of his words,
always had some pretty compliment at her
service, which, it is to be feared, the maiden
did not appreciate at the same value it would
have had if issued from younger lips, or concocted
beneath a less scant and hoary pate; for she only

favoured him with short replies, and pouted scornfully when he called her Rosebud, May-dew, and the like. They also encountered St. Barbe, still obtrusively polite, but looking a solitary, old, well-to-do man; for death had disencumbered him of his wife and family. He always told Nicholas Drew now that he envied him the possession of Adie. "But who," he would add, "who could foresee that of all his children not one would be left to him?" The Frenchman spoke, and passed on, but looked back often at the tall lithe figure quietly pacing along with Nicholas; he had been over-prudent, certainly, or she might have been his companion instead, he thought.

It was a calm, almost breathless, evening, but now the sun was gone the air was cool; a few red bars crossed the west, supported by broad masses of purple cloud; the low meadows by the river-side had just been mown, and the fresh hay gave out its pleasant healthy scent. Many persons, young men especially, were resting on the ground where it lay, some smoking, some talking, others enjoying the luxury of perfect idlesse. Amongst the last, Adie was the first to descry Laurence Royston. He sat apart from the rest, with a great, shaggy water-dog coiled up on the grass beside him. The animal had been in the river, and had run past Adie some time since, bestowing on her dress a plentiful sprinkling in his transit. Laurence Royston had seen this; and as Adie, with Nicholas Drew and the printseller, approached, he rose and offered an apology for his companion's misconduct. The next most natural thing to do was to join their party, and, walking beside Adie, to talk to her of the beauty of the evening, and the still loveliness of the twilight prospect—at least, he appeared to think so, for this was what he did.

"When the moon rises, it is more beautiful still," remarked Adie, looking towards the city, that is, towards the Minster.

"I do not like moonlight—it is so chilling, so pale; I have an antipathy to moonlight," said Royston, quickly.

Adie seemed surprised.

"You are going to ask me whence arises my antipathy. Well, I cannot tell you," added he;

"it is one of those indescribable feelings which afflict some people to the utter bewilderment of everybody else. They reiterate their why, why, when, if they would only take the trouble to look at home, they would remember, most probably, that they have themselves some dislike or loathing equally unreasonable."

Adie smiled, and a half-blush suffused her cheek, though it was becoming almost too dusk to see it; for she recollected some very strong but groundless enmities of her own.

"Have you balanced the account in your mind, and freed me from your first sentence of bad taste or foolishness?" asked Royston, quietly.

Instead of replying, Adie started a little to one side, then walked on rapidly in advance. Laurence Royston paused to see what had caused this movement, and observed a great toad crawling heavily under the hedge. He came quickly up to her again, when she turned, and said—

"Those cold-blooded creeping things make me thrill; I cannot bear them."

"Yet they are harmless; and the moonlight

makes *me* thrill too. I always exclude it from my rooms. If it shines upon my face when I am sleeping, I have bad dreams. My adversary in the picture you wot of, tempts me with some splendid prize to do evil deeds; or I am falling, falling, always falling over a precipice; or on water churned into white foam with fury, and only a plank between me and death; or I am destroying what I most love, and cursing myself as I do it."

The two, who had outwalked Nicholas and the print-dealer, were now summoned to return; and they all four sauntered slowly in company towards the city. Long before they reached it, the moon was up, and the water rippled all white in its cold light, while the clouds and the ruins of St. Servin's Abbey, and the Minster towers beyond, high up in the clear atmosphere, looked larger and ghostlier in its shimmering radiance. The young stranger had been silent for some minutes, when Adie asked archly, if the Tempter were discoursing with him then.

"No; I was holding a parley with my better angel," was the reply. "He has not forsaken

me quite; he is glad to find me in such good
company."

Adie spoke no more after that until they
stopped by the Minster gates to say good-night
to Marsh, who parted from them there. She
then asked, if he should go back to his lodging
at Crossley by the fields. No, he answered; he
had decided to remain in the town, and had
found other rooms more convenient for his business than those so far off. Nicholas, overhearing
this, invited him to return and sup with them,
as, being a stranger, he could not yet have many
friends. Royston acceded; and they crossed the
Minster yard as the great clock struck ten. The
court was extremely hushed when they entered
it, for all the early workpeople were quiet in
their rooms. Coming from the dark College
Lane, it seemed quite light, almost as if snow
lay on the flags and steps. They stopped a few
minutes to notice the fine effect of the quaintly
ornamented house in the moonshine, and then
mounted the stairway one by one. Martha
admitted them in her taciturn, down-looking, yet
observant way. She had been on the watch for

her master's return some time, and hearing
Royston's voice down in the court, had hastened
to open the door, while she knitted a few more
loops of the web. An oil lamp burnt on the
table in the centre of the room, but it scarcely
threw out light enough to fill its dusky corners;
for it was a spacious apartment, and had many
little niches and recesses. Through the uncurtained windows the slanting moonbeams streamed
down on the ledges and floor, but faded as they
came within the circle of the lamp. The farther
side of the room, where the oak closet was, and
the disused door which opened upon the common
staircase of the house, lay all in shadow, except
when one of the metal knobs on the panels
twinkled like an inquisitive eye in the gloom.
In taking his seat, Royston faced this part of the
room, and some inconsequential remark of his
led Nicholas to say there was no egress by that
way, for he had bolted the door up so many
years ago that rust must long since have riveted
it fast.

"There is a long passage just outside, which
the people say is haunted," observed Adie, smiling.

"It is haunted by footsteps; nothing is to be seen."

" I should imagine not," replied Royston, with a curious laugh. " But pray what sort of footsteps are they,—light and tripping, or with the orthodox tramp, tramp? I confess that it has always puzzled me why a ghost should have such solidity of step, when it is but an airy nothing. Describe this hapless soul's march; I should like to hear it, never having been so favoured."

"It is very slow and solemn, as of a person walking while he meditates, quite regular and never pausing. It only comes occasionally, in the dead of winter nights; at no other time. Mrs. Parkes has heard it, but I never have; Grizzie has too."

" Yes; I have heard strange sounds in this old house," added Nicholas, gravely; for his mind was deeply tinctured with superstition, and he did not like to hear these mysterious matters lightly spoken of. "I believe that was the real reason why I closed up the door, though I tried to persuade myself at the time it was because of the children's noise and rudeness."

" And what is the second door, the double one? does that also open on the corridor?" asked Royston.

" Oh, no; that is the closet where Grizzie keeps his treasures!" cried Adie, laughing; " even I have never been in there. It is the ghost's quarters perhaps. Grizzie, what is the legend of the footsteps?—do you know?"

The old engraver appeared somewhat annoyed at her abruptness.

" In that closet there is nothing that you or any one else would style treasures," said he; " but the footsteps appear to issue from it. The story goes that two brothers lived here formerly, who had united in the commission of a murder— the murder of a priest. The elder, to save himself, when the chase was hot after them, denounced his brother as the sole culprit, and betrayed where he might be taken, namely, in that oak closet; where, after the commission of the crime, he had hidden himself with his remorse. He himself paced the corridor, waiting for the people who were coming to seize his brother. The younger suffered death, and the elder walks there still, and will walk, probably, so long as Nevil's Court remains."

Laurence Royston smiled at the old man's credulity.

"I have small faith in such legends myself," said he; "but they assort well with the gloom and antiquity of these middle-age abodes. Indeed, they would scarcely be complete without their ghost. I should like to see the inside of that oak closet."

Adie expected to hear Nicholas refuse; but instead, he bade Royston bring the lamp, and he should be gratified. The doors being unlocked and thrown open, they all three stood within. The atmosphere was heated and airless; dust lay everywhere thickly, except on the old table and chair where the engraver had probably sat during the time he was shut up there in the evening. Spiders' webs festooned even the frames of these, and were woven in every available nook. A mark as of fingers over the lock of the ancient cabinet attracted Royston's notice.

"This is a fine piece of old workmanship; I never saw anything of the kind richer or more

elaborate," he observed. "Does the interior cor-
respond in beauty with the outside?"

"Yes; the drawers are inlaid with ivory,"
replied Nicholas; but he made no further movement to gratify his guest's curiosity.

"It is a remarkable looking cabinet," said
Royston, lingering before it still.

"You are right; it belonged to those miserable
brothers, and contained proofs of their guilt when
the one was taken. The footsteps start from it,
and go down the corridor and back again."

"Oh, Grizzie, and do you keep your treasures
in this wicked old cabinet?" asked Adie, half
alarmed, yet half laughing. "You will find them
changed into withered leaves and gray dust some
day."

"They are no better than dust now," replied
Nicholas. "Come out; you have seen enough."

Royston was standing at the window, from
which he had contrived to rub a little of the
accumulated dirt. He saw that it looked upon a
garden, and asked whose it was, and if Adie ever
walked there.

"No; it belongs to the people who live in the

old palace," said she, passing from the closet into
the room.

Nicholas had to stand two or three minutes
before his guest followed her, and then the door
was reclosed and locked. As he was returning
the key to his pocket, Royston asked to look at it.
It was a very curious, heavy, rude implement,
eaten with rust in round spots, as if blood had
fallen upon it.

" It is strong enough to keep out a legion of
ghosts," said he, weighing it in his hand. " They
do not make keys like this now-a-days; it seems
as if it had been formed to lock in deadly secrets
on which hung men's lives. I can imagine many
a plot having been hatched behind those ancient
doors, while this key was tightly held in nervous
fingers ; but it tells no tales."

As he spoke, the Minster clock struck eleven,
and Martha entered to bolt the door for the night.
Seeing Royston still there, she would have retired,
but her master bade her stop.

" You must go now," he added, addressing the
young man. " We keep early hours in the court.
Go gently."

Royston descended the creaking steps, and paused at the last to repeat his "Good night," which Adie echoed pleasantly as she stood at the doorway with Nicholas.

"Beware the fiend!" cried she, as he walked towards the gateway. "Say your prayers as you cross the Minster gardens; it is broad moonlight · still."

He turned round, laughing, and promised to obey; then disappeared under the shadow of the arch.

VI.

THE GHOSTLY FOOTSTEPS.

On every succeeding day throughout the months that followed this first visit, Laurence Royston was constant in his attendance on Nicholas Drew. He worked with diligence and success, notwithstanding the bright eyes that often overlooked him; and the old engraver was pleased and satisfied with his pupil. He was enthusiastic himself, and he thought Royston, under his cold cynicism, had sparks of the genial fire too. His coming also gratified Adie; for she liked change and variety, of which there was ordinarily but little in Nevil's Court.

It was not strange that after a while she grew to like him, because his manner towards her was impregnated with the subtlest flattery. He differed essentially from every one she knew, in his quiet ways of winning into and answering her unuttered thoughts. He made his mind, as it were, chime responsive to hers; he studied her face until he understood her feeling ere she could express it; he observed her tastes and distastes, her little whims, weaknesses, and vanities, and played upon them with a master-hand, until he could wind and turn her any way he would, and all this without having committed himself by a single word. He went through it like a game of skill, in which the most astute must win; while she blushed, and was angry and astonished at herself in secret to see how much she was giving for nothing—unasked, possibly undesired. She could not lay the soothing unction to her heart that Laurence Royston so much as liked her; for if he were kind, almost tender, one day, he would be cynical and careless the next; if his eyes dwelt on her caressingly one moment, the next there came over them that flickering sinister light as of a cruel thought shining through.

Nicholas, as they learnt to know each other better, began to regard him with less favour; *why* was not apparent; he distrusted him, probably. One dark November night, Adie happened to be left alone in the room at Nevil's Court; Nicholas had gone out reluctantly on business, and Martha had been absent a few days in the country, where she was supposed to have gone to nurse her aged mother. The girl sat idly by the crackling wood-fire, twirling in her fingers the shrivelled relics of the wild white rose, which she had fetched from its hiding-place to keep her thoughts company. In her eyes there was a deeper, stiller expression than formerly, and a less frequent smile on her lips also; but the rich glow of her southern beauty had not lost a single tint. Her heart was restless, but not sorrowing.

Laurence Royston had been there in the morning, in his pleasanter mood; and as Adie sat alone

by the fire, she was thinking within herself how
dull they should be when he was gone away.
She, at least, not Nicholas; for he had said that
day, with a vehement expression quite unusual
to him when Royston had left, " Adie, I do not
like that man; I have been deceived in him;"
and she had turned away, with a slightly angry
flush darkening her brow. If the old man had
struck her, it would have pained her less than
hearing him speak thus. For the first time in her
life, she felt resentful against poor Nicholas,—felt
as if he had injured her; and she let him go out
before her passion cooled. She was brooding over
it now, when a sound caused her to raise her face
and listen intently. In the corridor, outside the
wall, there went slow, distinct, measured steps;
she could have counted them. Her cheeks
blanched, and all the blood rushed back violently
to her heart; but she kept her place within the
broad light which the fire threw out upon the
floor. The steps advanced and receded thrice,
and died into indistinctness far beyond the room.
Adie's angry thoughts had been put to flight by
this; she longed excessively for Nicholas's return.

A few minutes after, her heart gave a throb of relief, for she heard some person mounting by the outside stairway. She rushed to the door, and opened it in haste, to admit, not the engraver, but Laurence Royston.

"There is nobody at home but myself," said she, in confusion at his sudden and unexpected appearance. "Grizzie has gone down into the Barbican."

She stood holding the latch in her hand, expecting him to depart; but he advanced into the room, and lifted his hat from his head, saying,—

"It is a wet night, Adie; give me an hour's shelter. Will he soon be back again?"

"Yes; he promised to hasten, as I was alone," she replied; and she shut the door, for the wind blew in coldly and strongly.

Royston stood by the fire, resting his arm upon the mantelshelf; Adie sat down in her old place, secretly wishing that the visit had been better timed, and feeling an inward conviction that Nicholas would be displeased to find his pupil there at his return.

"What is the matter, Adie?" asked Royston,

gently. "You look as if you had seen a ghost; such wild eyes and pale cheeks!"

"I have heard the footsteps to-night," replied she, looking up in his face. "I was wishing so much that Grizzie would come back when you arrived. I dare not be left alone again in the house."

"Silly Adie! I thought you had more courage than to tremble at a sound. What harm can those footsteps do you?"

"They make me nearly sick with fear; I should go mad if I heard them often; they make my blood cold in my veins; I cannot describe it. If you had not come, I should have gone down to Mrs. Parkes and Job until Grizzie came home."

"Now that I am here, Adie, let me speak to you: I have a word for your ear alone. Will you listen to me, Adie?"

Her colour came and went rapidly, for there was a passionate tenderness in his voice that she could not misunderstand; but an instinct of maidenly reserve whispered that he ought not to have sought her clandestinely, and stilled the rush of joy to her heart. She drew away her hand which he had taken, quietly and with a certain coldness, but she could not shroud the lustre in her eyes that belied the impulse.

" Adie," he repeated, earnestly,—" Adie, have you never seen my love for you? is my dear hope to fail? "

That strange voice of his had a truthful ring in it now he had left acting. A quick change passed over the girl's face; she put up her hand to shed back the long hair from her brow, and looked at him—openly, honestly, questioningly. Some doubt of him must have crossed her mind then, for he drew back before her glance, which expressed it.

" Adie, if I tried you, it was but to spare myself pain; I could not make my heart a football for a girl's caprice," he said, deprecatingly. " I did not know you until lately, and since then you have been all my thought. Forgive me, Adie, forgive me; at least, if you deny my love."

A thrill ran through Adie's frame as if a cold wind had breathed upon her, that quick convulsive shiver which is said to creep along the nerves when some step passes over the spot where our grave is to be made. She remembered Nicholas's few stern words that morning, and an indefinable sensation of fear, pain, and longing, stole into her heart. He saw the wavering, and was swift to turn it to account. Warm loving words, passionate vows, fell softly, dreamily, into the porches of her ears, and passed on to the responsive heart-chords, making them all musical with delight; the rosy blush deepened; the lustrous gleaming eyes grew humid, and her lips quivered into a confession.

"Then, Adie, you are mine—mine!" cried Royston, exultant; "you will not let any one separate us. I love you better than my life, and you must give me the same love; if you love me best of all, you will leave all for me."

Adie remembered poor Nicholas's kindnesses; and her tender conscience reproached her for deceiving him.

"Do you regret already?" said Royston; "do you fear I cannot hold my own? Keep our secret until I bid you speak, and all will be well; promise me this." Adie promised. "I shall come to-morrow. Now I will leave you, lest Nicholas should return. You are not afraid of the footsteps now, are you?"

" Oh, no," she replied, smiling.

But he lingered still—there were so many warm assurances and farewells to make, so many warnings to give; but at last he was gone, and Adie sat down again by the fire alone. Her mind was in a whirl, she saw nothing clearly; one sensation only was distinct, and that was painful,— she had given her word to deceive poor old Nicholas—confiding, honest old Nicholas; that was bad; it was wicked. She felt less happy than before Laurence Royston had said he loved her; what she had coveted so earnestly had brought the first dark stain upon her conscience. She tried to thrust the obtrusive self-reproach aside, but it refused to be banished. While she was thus at war with her better genius, the engraver came in. He had ascended the steps unheard, and appeared before her so unexpectedly, that she started and uttered a cry of alarm; which she explained by saying that she had heard the footsteps in the corridor soon after he had

left her, and that since every slight noise made
her tremble.

" The footsteps ? " repeated Nicholas, in a
troubled tone.

" Yes ; they came and went three times between
the closet and the stairs, and then ceased," said
Adie.

The old man stood before the fire in his wet
tartan, gazing sadly into the red caverns of the
embers.

" They have begun early this winter," he remarked. " What is it they forbode ? "

" Do you take them for an evil prophecy,
Grizzie ? " the girl asked, going to him affectionately, and disencumbering him of his drenched
cloak and hat.

" Yes, child, they have always proved such ;
but perhaps it may not be to you or me, but to
others in the house. Listen ! "

The regular echoing tramp came up the corridor
again. Adie trembled, as she clung to the old
man's arm ; the steps came nearer and nearer,—
threatening, angry steps they were. They tra-
versed the length of the corridor several times,

and then all was again still; Adie could hear the beating of her own heart in the hush that followed. Nicholas passed his hand gently over her head, which rested against his breast, saying, " God shield thee from harm, child! "

At that moment an impulse came strongly upon her to tell Nicholas what had passed during his absence; but a thought of Royston checked the confession on her tongue,—might he not be displeased with her?—so she held her peace, and withdrew herself from the kind arm which had been so long her protection. She went to the window, and looked out into the dense, blown, wintry night; there was a faint reflection on the wet pavement of the court from some fire in a room below, and her eye fixed on the glistening pools. It was not possible she could have been deceived, but she half doubted the evidence of her senses, when the figure of Laurence Royston emerged stealthily from the open doorway of the house, and, darkening the light for a moment, passed out at the arch into College Lane. She made no remark, but returned to the hearth; Nicholas was unlocking the doors of the oak closet. He went in alone, leaving them ajar, and presently called to her.

" Adie, did you or Laurence Royston observe where the cabinet stood last summer ? " he asked. " I have not been in here since I showed it to you both, and it seems to me that it has been thrust from the wall; it certainly stood close to it formerly."

The girl could not remember, but she went in and looked. " I did not notice that there was a door behind it, Grizzie, so it must have been moved, or I should certainly have seen it," said she. " Is the door locked up ? "

He shook it strongly, and replied, " Yes, it is fast; but the fastenings are without. The bolts are gone from the staples inside, and there is no key, unless the one that belongs to the outer door opens this also."

He fetched it and tried, but it turned in the wards without unlocking it. He made Adie repeat her description of the footsteps, and questioned her particularly as to whether she had heard any other noise, to which she replied that she had not.

"I will look further into the matter to-morrow," said the engraver, seriously. "We have little to lose, it is true; but evil-disposed persons have been known to make use of such legends as attach to this house in Nevil's Court for bad purposes. It is well to be on our guard. The cabinet has been moved from without; something has been introduced through the wide crevice between the door and the wall, and so it has been pushed forward."

That night both Nicholas and Adie lay long awake; the one listening for the footsteps, the other revolving the evening's occurrences with alternate thrills of joy and pain; but no sound disturbed the stillness, except the loud Minster clock and the gusts of sighing winter wind.

The following morning Nicholas rose early, long before Adie was awake, and went down into the court, and thence by the common stair into the corridor. He carried with him a lantern, and narrowly examined the floor, which in the thick dust showed traces of feet backwards and forwards. This circumstance convinced him that some actual person had occasioned the previous

night's alarm, and that it was not the ghostly
visitant Adie had heard. He tried the door of
the closet, but could not stir it; and then returned
to his room, where he applied himself as quietly
as possible to undoing the closed-up entrance from
it to the corridor. This was a work both of time
and difficulty, and it was still undone, when he
heard Adie moving in her room; he immediately
desisted, and, lest she should be troubled by needless alarms, he made everything look as much
like what it did before as possible. After breakfast he fetched a blacksmith, and had the cabinet
secured to the wall of the closet by several strong
staples; it then completely covered the door, and
made an entrance by that means next to an impossibility.

Royston came while the man was at work, and
expressed his approval of Nicholas's precautions;
he afterwards examined the corridor with him,
and suggested that the door into it should be
opened, that the nocturnal visitant might be
detected. The engraver privately told him
what he was doing, but said Adie must not
know, or she would be in a constant tremor

and excitement. Laurence promised to repeat nothing.

After that day the engraver never left Adie alone in the house; Martha returned; and the weeks crept on until nearly Christmas. The footsteps were heard no more, and the first impression of alarm died away; Nicholas even began to talk of once more closing up the door, because it admitted draughts; but the doing of it was deferred from day to day, until it was forgotten again. But one black moonless night, as the engraver lay awake, he heard a sound passing by the wainscot that caused him to start up in haste. It was of a stealthy, naked foot, and a hand drawn along by the wall as if feeling the way. He passed into the large room, and succeeded in opening the door noiselessly; but when he flashed his' light into the corridor, it was silent and empty, only a rush of wind sweeping up it extinguished his candle. He went no more to bed, but sat listening and expectant; but the visitant, whether of flesh and blood, or of shadow and spirit, came not again.

This time he did not think fit to speak of what

he had heard to any one. However, Martha, whom nothing escaped, had been startled by the same noise, and had moreover seen with wonder a figure that she well knew steal across the court shortly after. In the winter nights a lighted oil lamp hung inside the gateway of the court. Now possibly that secret visitant had not calculated that there were such wakeful eyes and such industrious thoughts upon his track as Martha's discovery entailed. Her web, which had hitherto run tolerably straight, was all at once thrown into inextricable entanglement.

VII.

CHRISTMAS EVE.

CHRISTMAS EVE came; a loud blustrous day, with a light covering of snow upon the ground, and clouds heavy with storms in the sky. Laurence Royston had left Eversley for a few days, saying, that he intended to spend the festive season with some relatives at a distance. Adie was sorrowful during his absence; for she had still to bear the

burden of her secret, and to deceive old Nicholas.
Her treachery weighed on her heart; but though
she had entreated Royston to let her tell him,
he had always put her off, saying, that such a
confession would lead to their instant separation;
for the engraver was resolute in his way, and
had evidently conceived a strong distaste for his
pupil's character. Since they had become better
acquainted, Royston had let fall much of his
disguise, and had frequently given utterance to
hard, selfish, worldly principles that had revolted
the good old man; and detecting, in spite of their
guarded manner, that he and Adie were on closer
terms than they wished to appear, Nicholas had
pressed forward his instructions, that there might
be no reason for the young man's remaining in
the town. But what most deeply grieved him
was, that Adie should have withheld her confidence from him. He turned it over in his mind,
and could not remember that he had ever given
her a harsh word that should make her fear him ;
and yet from her tone, and from her anxious
air and watchfulness, he knew she was keeping
something from his knowledge. Besides, coming

suddenly from the inner room one day into that
where he had left them together, he saw Royston
leaning over the girl's chair, winding her long
dark tresses round his fingers, and whispering to
her softly; he even bent over her, and kissed her
without resistance. At first, Nicholas thought he
would charge her with deception; but remembering her passionate resentment when thwarted, he
put it off, hoping that she would soon, of her own
accord, tell him all.

But he spoke to Royston in plain terms, telling
him that his visits in Nevil's Court must be discontinued, and that he had done a vile wrong in
poisoning the girl's mind against her protector,
so that she had learnt to deceive him. High and
angry words were exchanged between the two
men; but neither of them chose to make Adie a
party to the dispute. Royston doubted not that
he should succeed with her whenever he chose
to bring the matter to an issue, since her love for
him had already undermined old feelings of affection and gratitude; and Nicholas hoped that the
girl's own eyes would be opened by and by to
the real character of her lover. Things were in

this position when Royston left Eversley, just before Christmas. Perhaps Martha alone had a complete view of all that passed, for her watch never relaxed.

It was after dinner on Christmas Eve that Nicholas and Adie, sitting by the fire, both of them unoccupied, first felt how wide the gulf that lay between them had become. The unnatural restraint galled both, but neither could or would break it down. The old man was silent and mournful; Adie's thoughts yearned to comfort him; she longed to put her arms about Grizzie's neck, and to pull his beard, and hear him call her pet names as he used to do; but one re-membrance of the absent Royston tied her down to her chair. At length some allusion recalled the Christmas Eve long ago, when the engraver had taken the little child from the winter night into the shelter of his poor but warm hearth. Could that tall beautiful girl be the small, help-less, frozen thing that might have died in the snow unheeded but for him? and was this dis-tance and estrangement to be the sole reward of his charity? Perhaps in all his solitude the

old man had never felt more desolate or more
lonely than now, because the heart that he had
striven so long to bind to himself was turned
from him. He looked at her questioningly when
she was not observant, and saw that in her face
which told him she was not happy, as she had
been, or as she ought to be, and he experienced
a feeling of intense wrath against Royston as its
cause.

When the Minster bell began to ring for
prayers, Adie rose wearily from her chair, and
said she would go to the service. She did not
ask for Nicholas's company as she used to do,
but donned her bonnet and cloak, and went out
alone. When she had got into College Lane, her
heart smote her with the reproach that this was
not kind, and, turning hastily back, she re-
ascended the stairway to the room. The engraver
had pushed back his chair, and sat with his arms
on the table, and his face buried in them.
Adie, with quick remorse, sprang towards him,
crying—

"Oh, Grizzie, Grizzie, don't be grieved with
me ; let me tell you all ; let us be friends,

as we were before Laurence Royston came to Eversley."

The old man lifted up his head, and held forth his arms; she nestled into them, and began to weep passionately on his breast.

" Adie, child, why did you ever mistrust me? " said Nicholas. " Was I not always kind to you? would I not have almost coined my flesh into gold to have purchased you a pleasure? "

She only sobbed the more at the gentle rebuke of his tone.

" Adie, you love this bad man—nay, do not leave me—you love him? "

She did not answer, but wept on.

" You should have suspected him when he tempted you to deceive me. Who but a bad, treacherous man would have played his part? If he had come to me openly and honourably, I would have given you to him; but he must needs steal you away from your best friend. It was not honest, Adie; it was cruel and unjust— the act of a base, creeping nature. He was never, in his best days, worthy of you, my child; how much less, then, now, when he is all sullied with his crooked ways through the world—calloused, faithless, and, though you may not see it, cruel too!"

Adie had withdrawn herself from his encircling arm, and stood aloof, still tearful, but indignant too.

"Oh, Grizzie, you do not know him!" she said, with passionate force. "He is kind and gentle; he has never spoken one hard word of you; he would have told you weeks since, but he knew you did not like him, and we dreaded that you would command us to part."

"Adie, it was an evil day that brought him over our threshold; you will live to rue it. Oh, my heart's darling, I would let you go to him this instant, if I did not see such ominous shadows about his future. He is a wicked, evil man, and he will drag you down with him. It would have been better to have let you perish in the snow ten years ago, than to give you to him now."

Adie stood silent; the glistening tears hung on her lashes, but ceased to fall; a bright spot burnt on her cheek, but her passion cooled.

"Grizzie, will you hear him speak for himself?"

she said, tremulously; " I cannot plead our cause with you, for it makes my heart burn to hear such words against him from you. But you do not know him, or you would speak far other-wise."

" I will give him a fair hearing, my child. But do not let anything cause this cold shade between us to come back. Is this love of a few weeks to obliterate the memory of ten years, Adie ? "

" No, Grizzie, no ; I always wished you to know, and it was only because you were deceived that I was not perfectly happy," cried the girl, warmly. " Let us be friends."

Nicholas sighed, and fondly stroked the bright head that had again nestled against his breast ; but he said no more about Laurence Royston.

The Minster bells had ceased for several minutes, when the old man reminded her whither she had been going :

" Run away, my child ; you will still be in time for the beautiful anthem," said he.

She asked him to go with her ; but he said no, the evening was very cold, and he should

take so long wrapping up that the music would
be over; and, besides, he would rather sit by
the fire until she came back.   So she put her
two arms round his neck, kissed him, and went
to the door.   There for a minute she hesitated,
then turned back quickly to where Nicholas
stood, and said, with glittering eyes,—

"Grizzie, have you quite, *quite* forgiven me
my wickedness to you?"

"My darling, from my heart."

He blessed her and bade her go.

For a few minutes after Adie had left him,
Nicholas sat by the fire thinking of her pityingly
and with great love, as one blinded and mis-
guided by a most unhappy passion.   He folded
his hands, closed his eyes, and laid his head
back wearily, but not despondently.   "She will
come to see him clearly soon; only give her
time," said he to himself.   Then he rose, and
walked to and fro in the room, talking to himself, while his eyes took a softer gleam, and his
brow looked less stern than usual.   Perhaps he
was praying for his darling, for he went to the

window and gazed up eagerly to the stormy sky, as if invoking help or comfort for them both.

At last he lighted his lamp, and, entering the oak closet, unlocked the ancient cabinet, and proceeded to turn over the poor treasures it contained. Whilst thus occupied, he was startled by the sound of the opening door, and Laurence Royston's voice asking—

"Are you at home, Nicholas Drew?"

The young man was already in the closet; but Nicholas motioning him back, they both retired to the fireside.

"I thought you were far away from this. What brings you here to-night of all nights?" asked the engraver, impatiently.

"My own restless spirit, Nicholas," was the reply. "Where is Adie? Gone to say her prayers?"

"Yes; she is at the Minster."

"I have walked far, and I have walked fast; for it was like living in hell, that horrible suspense," said Royston, with grim earnestness. "I must have another answer from you about Adie. Old man, your blood runs slow; you know not what love is." He warmed up into passion, and those restless fingers of his clasped and unclasped themselves, clutching at the air.

Nicholas looked him steadily in the face, in nowise intimidated by Laurence's violence.

" I have nothing to add to what I said before," replied he.

This calmness seemed only the further to excite the young man.

" If I lose my soul for her, I will have her," said he, in a deep, suppressed tone, as if he were struggling to keep down a fierce gust of passion that was almost too strong for him. " You have hated me and suspected me for no cause but your own fancies; you have watched us, and divided us, and tried to turn her heart from me under a false, specious guise of affection. You have acted treacherously by her——"

The old man, roused out of his habitual meekness, confronted his accuser with an indignant, steady gaze.

" It is you—*you*, Laurence Royston—who have played the traitor in this house!—you, with lying words, have poisoned her good heart. She has

told me all; and, by the God above us, if gratitude and affection have any power remaining,
your wife she will never be. Your evil influence
has not done all its work; she will *not* forsake
me; she will come to know you as you are. Go
out of my sight! Adie shall never, with my will,
see your wicked face again."

While he was thus speaking, Laurence, with
his teeth set, and lurid eyes burning, stood
irresolute; but as Nicholas waved him towards
the door, his wild suppressed passion broke
bounds; and pressing on the old man, he took
from his breast a pistol, which he had carried for
his protection on the journey, and shot him dead.
The moment the deed was done, he started as if
the tempting and now triumphant devil had
laughed in his ear; and stooping hastily down, he
clutched the dabbled white hair in his gloved
hand, and raising the ghastly face, saw that he
had done his murderous work but too surely.
For five hideous minutes he stood beside the
corpse staring at it. O God, with what awful
thoughts! Lifting his hat to wipe off the heavy
beads of sweat from his face, his cheek was

touched by the clammy glove; he could scarcely
repress a shriek, and dragging it from his hand—
that hand which could never lose its stain of
blood-guiltiness—he flung it far from him on the
floor. Presently came the idea of escape—imme-
diate escape; and his mind, used to quick con-
ception and prompt action, in an instant devised
it simply and safely. He first secured the door
into the court, and then, going into the closet,
he flung about upon the floor the contents of the
cabinet, to give the appearance of the old man's
having met his end from robbers who, attracted
to his dwelling by the fabulous rumours of his
wealth, had broken in upon him, and, meeting
with resistance, had killed him for the sake of
plunder. This done, he returned to his poor
victim, and stayed by him, biting his nails, and
with his awful face darkened by fear, remorse,
and despair, for some time. Hearing a light step
in the court, which he knew well, he flung his
arms wildly into the air, and, opening the door
into the disused and haunted corridor, he plunged
into its darkness, and made his escape, leaving
his glove—that guilty witness—on the floor.

It was a cold misty twilight abroad, with heavy gusts of wind driving round corners and sweeping the snow from the ledges and drip-stones of the Minster. Adie gathered her cloak tightly about her, and feeling happier in mind than she had felt for many a day, entered the solemn gloom of the great church. She passed up one of the side aisles and by the steps to the altar-rails, where she was alone and almost in darkness. The few scattered lights showed her the congregation below in the choir, but so dimly that their presence was no company to her, and no disturbance. It was a luxury of enjoyment to her impressible character to linger in this solitude, thinking her own thoughts, dreaming her own dreams; and when the swell of the rich music rolled up to the vaulted roof, her heart seemed filled to overflowing with an ecstacy of devotion that was almost pain. The fall and rise of the symphony, and the sweet distant voices, were softened to her by her remote position; the proclamation fell on her ear as if out of heaven, " Peace on earth, and good will towards men ! "

" Oh, I am glad I told dear Grizzie, and that he forgave me," she thought to herself. " How

could I have borne to listen to this, if I were
deceiving him still? Good, kind old Grizzie, it
was very cruel of me; how could I do it, even
for Laurence?"

She stayed until the last, until the people, and
priests, and choristers had vanished, and the
vergers came to put out the lights; then she
slowly left the Minster, and issued out into the
night.

The wind had increased to a tempest, and drove
furiously about the open space. If it had been
light enough, you would have almost expected to
see it careering madly with outspread vaporous
wings in the shaken air. She could scarcely keep
her feet against it, and often the gusts caught her,
compelling her to stand still for a minute to regain
strength and breath; then there came shrill
shrieking blasts which seemed to warn her back,
followed by long piteous wails and moans and
laments, that died into a momentary hush only to
be renewed again and yet again. At last, she
reached the comparative calm of the court, and
paused a little while, thinking within herself that
it was on just such a night as this that Grizzie had

found her crouched under the archway, crying for her father. Good old Grizzie! She looked up to the windows, hoping to see his figure darkening the glow from within; but the ruddy firelight shone through full and unbroken. She mounted the steps softly, intending to surprise him and reproach him archly for not keeping watch for her return, scarcely expecting, however, that she should reach the door before it would be opened; but she did, and peering cautiously through the glass, as soon as her eye became accustomed to the light, she saw that something unusual had happened. The doors of the closet stood open, and there was a candle on the table within; there was also a heap of things lying about the floor, but Nicholas was not visible.

"Perhaps he is at the cabinet, or sitting in the corner by the fire," said Adie to herself, though her heart throbbed fast and painfully. She attempted to open the door; but it was fastened inside, and resisted all her efforts. Then her alarm was aroused; for it was not customary with Nicholas to lock the door when he was in until night. She knocked loudly on the glass, and

cried, " Grizzie, Grizzie, let me in ; it is
Adie."

There was no answer but the echoes of her own
voice. She ran down the steps in haste, and to
Mrs. Parkes's door ; but that also was shut, for
Job and his wife had gone to spend their Christmas
Eve abroad. The whole court seemed deserted ;
even the children had vanished. Where could
Martha be? she was not used to go out so late.
Then Adie remembered that she had asked leave
to spend the afternoon at the hospital with an old
acquaintance, and she had not returned yet. The
girl, now full of fears and excitement, ran into
College Lane, in the hope of meeting some neighbours. A tall figure enveloped in a cloak rushed
by her, and was lost instantly in the pitchy darkness. The person had come out of the court, and
must have emerged from the stairway, for she
had not seen him before; but his sudden and
hasty appearance now redoubled her terror. At
this moment Martha came up; Adie caught her
by the arm, and whispered faintly that something
must be wrong, for she had left home not an
hour before, and now she could not get in. The

woman mounted the stair swiftly, and looked through the glass, with the girl close behind her.

"The door into the corridor is open; we must go that way," said she, after vainly trying to make herself heard by rattling the window.

They descended again, and went up the black, broken stair, feeling their way. When they entered the long passage, they perceived by the thread of light shining through a chink 'at the farther end that they were right in thinking the door was ajar. Adie, trembling in every nerve, clung fast to Martha, and relaxed her haste; she feared she scarce knew what.

There was a dead breathless silence within. They stood a moment and listened. No sound except the draught of the fire and the howling wind in the bishop's gardens. They went in, Martha the first. Nicholas lay prostrate across the hearth, his face downwards, one arm outstretched. A dark slender stream had trickled down the slope of the floor almost to where their feet had been arrested by the sight. Adie stood petrified with horror; Martha advanced, and stooped down over the old man. He was dead—

murdered; a small hole in the left temple betrayed
how.

They heard steps below in the court; Adie
rushed frantically to the door, and drawing back
the bolts, called to two men who were there to
come up in haste. The tale spread, and in a few
minutes, as it seemed, Mrs. Parkes and Job were
there, and Mr. St. Barbe, and many others, all
talking in awed whispers, which rose at times to a
hoarse scream. Adie watched helplessly, and
listened, and turned her dusk, clouded, distraught
eyes from one face to another, as if questioning
whether it were a dream or a reality. She did
not dare to look on the dead still countenance yet;
and when they carried the corpse into the next
room, she did not follow, but stayed by the fire,
which was sparkling and roaring in the keen
frosty air with a living mocking lustre. She
picked up a glove from the floor, and twitched
it nervously and unconsciously in her fingers, and
gazed about the floor, and then crept to the other
room, and stood behind Martha and Mrs. Parkes,
trembling and fearful, but with dry burning
eyes.

The idle marvel-mongers were dismissed, and then the officers, who had arrived in the interval, took note of the appearance of the first room. One of them said, " The old man must have been shot by some one who took him at advantage; there has been no struggle; he has been murdered for the purposes of robbery."

They went into the closet. The cabinet was open, the drawers out, and their contents scattered on the table, the floor, and in the adjoining room. They were a miscellaneous collection; women's clothes and a few valueless trinkets, child's things, and toys,—the poor old miser's treasures. There was nothing else left,—probably had been nothing else to leave,—so the man-slayer was disappointed of his spoil. The people looked at the yellow linen and tarnished bits of jewellery with curiosity; and Mrs. Parkes observed that somebody must have done *it* who knew the house well and Nicholas also,—somebody who believed the old story that he kept money hid away in that closet. For her part, she had long known it to be all nonsense, but there *were* folks who credited it. Martha spoke not a word, but peered about for traces in

her furtive eager way ; there was a set rigidity in
her face, as if she had registered a vow of vengeance and were seeking the way to its accom-
plishment. Her search was abortive, however,
and for the present she discontinued it to listen to
what Mrs. Parkes was saying about the murdered man.

"Who would have thought it of old Nicholas
Drew?" she was asking. "Who would have
thought he would have set such store by a lot of
rags? They are dropping with age,—look!" and
she lifted one of the garments from the floor, and
held it up. "Whose can they have been?"

"His young wife's and his bairn's," answered
Job.

"His wife's, Job? I never knew he had been
married," cried Mrs. Parkes, softly, but with
vivid curiosity.

"It was before your time; but I remember
her. A pretty, dark-haired little lass she was,
and very kind-spoken to poor folks. They were
well off then, I daresay; but they were very
young to be married, everybody said. Then
they had a bairn, and I know both she and it died

in a fever; and after that Nicholas was out of his mind ever so long, and had to be taken care of. When he came back to live in the court, he had let his beard grow, and was so queer, people were half afraid of him; and then it was they began to set stories afloat about his being a miser and a wizard, and what not."

Adie heard this little explanation of poor Grizzie's treasures, and with a melancholy reverence she gathered them together, and put them back into the drawers. Whilst doing so a folded paper slipped from between two handkerchiefs; she opened it, and saw coiled round and round a thick tress of black hair with a little auburn curl lying upon it. Then her tears began to flow, gently at first, but soon in wild passionate sobs and writhing. The women carried her away to her own chamber, and shut themselves up together, while one of the officers and St. Barbe stayed in the outer room. Before morning broke, the girl was raving in delirium, calling on "Laurence, Laurence!"

"Who is it she wants?" asked Mrs. Parkes of Martha. "We had better send for him maybe."

" He is not in the town now, and I don't know where he is either. He went away for his Christmas," was the reply. " It is Laurence Royston."

" See, poor thing, she has got one of his gloves, and she's holding it against her heart," said the other, with tears. " Poor Adie! Oh, it's an awful deed! I do hope, though it isn't Christian-like perhaps,—I do hope whoever did it will be brought to justice. He was a very good old man."

" He *was* good," repeated Martha, emphatically'; " and I will never rest day nor night until the man that did it is dead—never ! "

She spoke in a deep, concentrated, ireful voice, which made the calmer Mrs. Parkes shiver.

The girl's pitiful cry and moan went on still. They tried to calm her :

" Yes, Adie, he is coming,—he is coming soon," said Mrs. Parkes, laying her hand on the burning forehead, which turned restlessly on the pillow.

Adie opened her eyes with a start, and put up her arms as if to push away some weight; the glove fell to the floor, and was picked up by Martha, who laid it carefully in one of her young mistress's drawers, thinking that she set great store by it. Presently she grew quiet, and sank into a heavy sleep, which even the loud pealing of the Christmas-morning bells could not break, while a few paces off lay the dead cold clay which had shrined a soul then in God's Paradise.

VIII.

" WITH WIND AND RAIN."

THEY buried Nicholas Drew in the churchyard of St. Mark's, just without Friargate. The search after his murderer was prolonged for weeks, but no clue could be found, and speculation exhausted itself without discovering any adequate explanation of the foul crime.

" Wait," said Martha, " wait. We shall live to see him punished yet. The blood of murdered men will not sink into the ground until the hand that spilt it is cold."

It was a dismal winter. Adie lay long, hovering between life and death; sometimes quiet and

forgetful, at others roused by a shuddering re-
membrance of the awful scene she had witnessed.
St. Barbe would have removed her to his own
house; but, with a singular pertinacity, she clung
to Nevil's Court and refused to leave it; even the
entreaties of Laurence Royston, who had returned
to Eversley at the first summons, failed with her
in this instance. He was very faithful and constant in his attendance upon her; and when she
at last issued forth from her chamber, and took
short walks in the open air, he was invariably
her companion. Winter was merging into spring,
when, supported by his arm, she tottered down
the stairway for the first time. There was a
tender April shining in the sky, no clouds, no
wind, and a fresh warm air. They stood a few
minutes in the Court with Mrs. Parkes, and then
went out into College Lane.

"Which way shall we go, Adie? By the river-
side?" asked Royston.

"No; to Grizzie's grave. I have not seen it
yet," she replied.

Laurence remonstrated with her, but ineffec-
tually; so they turned towards Friargate. Many

people knew the poor girl in her trailing black garments, and with her mournful face, and gave her a word in passing of kindness and encouragement: doubtless they suspected the pious errand on which she was bound. The iron gate into the churchyard stood open, for a wedding-party had just gone in, so Adie and Laurence entered alone. The grave had been made close to the footpath, the rank grass already covered it with greenness, and a plain stone, with the name and age, had been put up at the head. They stood by it a few minutes in silence; but the place was very public, and curious observers were gathering, both in the porch and about the gateway, to see the bride and bridegroom issue from the church. Adie turned away with a deep sigh.

"When I am here, Laurence, I do not long for revenge so much," said she; "but sometimes I feel as if I could kill whoever murdered Grizzie with my own hands. Do you think God will let him go free always?"

Royston evaded a direct reply, and tried to turn her thoughts into another channel; but he was hurried and confused himself, and, after a

few disconnected sentences, he became silent.
They took their way out into the country,
amongst the fields and hedgerows, which were
changing their black winter robes for a green and
purplish hue: the birds twittered in their nests,
and all living nature seemed lifted up and vivified
by the warm breathing spring.

Royston returned to the subject of Adie's leaving
Nevil's Court, and urged it vehemently.

"You will never be happy in that haunted old
house," said he; "you will dwell on your miserable recollections until your mind is quite un-
hinged. Be guided, Adie; go down south with
me. Will you?"

He looked anxiously into her face, but she made
a negative gesture.

"I cannot, Laurence. It would be ungrateful
to poor Grizzie; as if I were in haste to forget
him. No, I must stay here with Martha until
something is discovered——"

"Nothing ever *will* be discovered," said Royston, abruptly. "Is it probable? every search
has been made—and, besides, there is no trace to
go upon."

" No matter; I can *wait*, as Martha says. The day *must* come."

Adie spoke with a quiet, assured confidence, which annoyed Royston excessively. He was in earnest to carry his point, and tried on another tack.

" My darling," said he, in his most dulcet voice, " how are you to exist? "

Adie made no reply to this question, but the hot tears gushed to her eyes at the insinuation it conveyed. Laurence gave the impression time to sink into her mind; but when she spoke at last, it was very differently from what he had anticipated.

" I can work when I will," were her words; " and if you leave me, Laurence, it will be all I shall have to think of."

" But how can I leave you, Adie? You know I cannot; you know I never shall."

The humid lustre disappeared from the girl's eyes, and a shadowy pallid smile came back to her lips.

" Let me take you away for a few months," persisted Royston, " to some pleasant sea-side

village, where you may regain your strength and
tone. Afterwards, if you are still bent on returning to Nevil's Court, I promise you faithfully
that you shall do it."

Adie shook her head.

" I have another plan. Let us go to the south
of France—to your father's and mother's country
—to your own birthplace—oh, that is beautiful!
Listen, Adie: it is a warm, soft, sunshiny country
—warm and sunshiny as your heart and face
were the first time I saw you. I must have
you look as you did then—all spirits and
beauty."

The temptation was very great; her resolution
began to waver.

" And you would bring me back, Laurence,
whenever I thought I *must* come ? "

" Yes, Adie; I promise it by what I hold most
dear—by our mutual love."

She was satisfied.

They were to be married in a few weeks, it
was agreed; for Adie had now no protector but
Laurence, and he urged the uselessness of delay.

On the eve of her wedding she lay awake long,
and many times during the night she roused
herself up to listen for the footsteps which she
fancied she heard in the corridor; but when she
bent her ear attentively to the sound, it always
resolved itself into either the creaking of a door
or the sighing of the wind amongst the trees.
Mrs. Parkes as well as Martha were in the room
with her; the first sleeping in an easy-chair, the
second keeping watch with an open Testament
before her, which had been her master's gift.
Spread out on a long couch at one side of the
chamber, were the bridal clothes: black, all
black; Adie would wear nothing else. Martha
glanced from her book to them, and from them
to the girl, who had fallen into an unquiet sleep,
and lay moaning as if in pain. A strange suspicion darted into her mind, and fastened there
beyond her power to expel it, though she tried
to do so. She fell into a reverie which lasted
some time; then she went to the wardrobe, and
opening a drawer where her mistress kept her
little valuables, proceeded to turn over its contents carefully. There was a shrivelled stalk

with a few colourless, crushed leaves and petals
clinging to it still.   It was not of that she was
in search, and it was laid cautiously aside to be
replaced.   At last, from the further corner, she
drew forth a glove of dark leather; a left-hand
glove, smelling of gunpowder, and with a stain
upon the forefingers as if they had clutched
something wet with blood.   Martha paused doubt-
fully.   Should she abstract it at once, or wait
for some link of connection?   It proved nothing;
she turned it over and over, examined its make
and the name of the manufacturer inside, and
registered its appearance in her mind; then it
and the other articles were laid back cautiously,
and she returned to her place.   Her countenance
was full of heaviness, her eyes of gloom; she
peered restlessly around, but avoided Adie's face,
and fixed only on the funeral-wedding garments.
She was debating a point in her own mind—
thinking of the kind master who had saved her,
and who loved the sleeping girl like his own
soul—what to do.   All at once there came over
her troubled spirit a long-forgotten sentence:
"'Vengeance is Mine; *I* will repay, saith the

Lord.' To Him it shall be left, then," said Martha, as if answering a voice that had spoken with her, and she addressed herself again to her reading in more tranquil mood.

The first sound that Adie heard when she awoke at dawn was the dashing of heavy rain and hail against the glass, and the loud hollow roar of a tempestuous wind. The weather had changed since the night before; and when she rose she shivered with cold from head to foot. Mrs. Parkes told her that Laurence Royston had come, and was waiting for her in the next room; therefore she made haste to don her sombre robes, and went out to him.

He started when he saw her, and exclaimed, in a tone of mingled surprise and reproach,—

" Adie, why this unseemly dress? You might give me your thoughts for to-day at least."

She coloured slightly, but repressed the tears that sprang to her eyes when she answered—

" Laurence, I dare not pass by poor Grizzie's grave decked out gaily; it would be cruel. I could not do it."

Royston uttered an impatient ejaculation; then,

seeing how deeply she was pained by his displeasure, and softened, too, by her exceeding beauty, he took her hands in his, and said he would try to forgive her; but it was hard that she should place anything before him then in her heart. She could neither smile nor brighten; she even shuddered as his cold fingers clasped hers, and tried to draw them away. They were standing on the hearth, and she had just looked down on the floor. She saw, or fancied she saw, upon the oak the murderous stain, and started away. A slight spasm convulsed Royston's features for a minute; he looked up, and he observed Martha watching them furtively from the chamber door. When she perceived herself detected, she disappeared. In an instant he was himself again— calm, resolute, and self-possessed.

He had attired himself in a rich new suit, with ruffles of fine foreign lace at the hands and breast, and looked, as Mrs. Parkes observed, a very "sightly man." Though it was the mode of the day, he wore no powder, but had his tawny hair in its natural waves and hue. He looked from himself to Adie, thinking that, if he could have suspected her whim, his dress should have accorded more with hers; but there was no time for any change then. Matters were compromised, however, by throwing over his gay coat a long dark cloth cloak, which in that inclement weather looked more suitable than finery.

St. Barbe was the only person who accompanied them, and when he reached the court and saw Adie, his astonishment and remonstrances exceeded Royston's. He would scarcely let her go; he said the rain was a bad omen, but the mourning garments were worse. She was not, however, to be stirred from her purpose; and the old Frenchman reluctantly yielded to her fantasy, but with many a shake of his head, and many a muttered prognostic of evil.

They were married at St. Mark's. Probably a stranger bridal party never entered the ancient church of the Friars. People gathered, as they always do on such occasions; but they looked as solemn as if they were attending a funeral, and whispered to each other about the incongruous appearance of the bride and bridegroom; for Royston was flushed and nervous, and Adie stood like a statue, and went through the ceremony mechanically. It was a singular sight; the gossips of the parish long remembered that marriage, as well they might; for it is not often such a pair come to be "joined together before God." When they emerged from the church porch, the little children were all mute; either the pelting rain had subdued their spirits, or else they felt that their shrill gratulations would be out of place. In passing Grizzie's grave, Adie suddenly stooped down, and snatched a handful of the wet grass which grew upon it, and thrust it into her bosom. Royston thrilled, and whispered a remonstrance, to which she gave no heed. She was thinking of the poor old man, who lay there unable to bless her. Would he bless her from heaven? she thought; and her heart answered, "No."

IX.

BY THE SOUTHERN SEA.

ADIE was happy, for Laurence was never absent from her, and in his presence her mind ceased to revert to painful things. They lived in a species of ecstatic dream, for themselves and for each other, without a thought of the indifferent outer world. All around them was calculated to substantiate and maintain this dream—the soft, warm climate, the romance-breathing country, and the lonely sea. They had established themselves in a little white cottage near the shore. It was enclosed by a shadowy old garden engirt by a low wall; and as they were strangers in a strange place their privacy was never intruded upon. The woman who acted as their servant, and to whom the cottage belonged, was as little unlike a machine as it is possible for a human being to be.

They had nothing to do all the livelong day but to stroll along the shore, watching the waves

and fishing-boats, and the cloud-shadows flitting
over the sea. Sometimes Laurence brought out
his pencil and made a sketch of the attractive bits
of coast scenery; but it was soon thrown aside
for a pleasanter occupation,—teasing or petting or
coaxing Adie, whose pretty coquettish ways and
frank gaiety had returned with her health and
glowing loveliness. There might have been but
these two in the world from the manner of their
life; they forgot everything else in their selfish
happiness, and took their enjoyment in the swift
present without one prescient forward glance.

Were they fools or wise? Moralists say the
present alone is certain. We will allow, then,
that they were wise with the wisdom of to-day in
their fool's paradise.

They had been out in a boat on the sea all the
summer day, and at sunset they were together
under the vine-covered veranda of the cottage,
both weary and both silent. It was a luxurious
calm. In the small, terraced garden, the slender-
leaved acacias swayed slowly and noiselessly in
the air, as if courting the sunbeams to toy with
them a little longer; a voluptuous mingling of

rich flower-odours suffused the atmosphere as with perfumed sighs of regret for parting day; while the sea blushed red and creamy rose as the lordly sun sank down upon its swelling bosom. On Adie's face there was the peace of full content; her soul expanded in the genial air of her own land, while her heart was satisfied with Royston's love—not *love*, perhaps, so much as passionate worship. There is no saying how it might have stood the tests of time and custom; but the present was sufficient for her—if it would always have stayed. There was no doubt in her mind that it could ever be otherwise with them; that Laurence would ever be otherwise than tender, or she otherwise than fond and foolish for his dear sake. No words can fitly describe her rapture, her enthusiasm of admiration for him; he was her god. The old affectionate gratitude for Grizzie was, in comparison, as a faint moonbeam to a tropical sun. Her southern heart set no stint to its idolatry; if her life could have profited him, she would with exquisite happiness have exhaled it in sighs upon his lips. He knew it, and he paid her for it in such coin as he had to give;

not in the virgin gold of an unselfish first love,
freshly coined in the mint of a good true heart,
but with a specious counterfeit which would last
its day, and pass undetected if it were not tried in
the furnace, or subjected to long wear and tear.
He *thought* he loved her; and so he did, at least
as well as he was capable of loving.   But is there
anything left in the hearts of these cynical cal-
culating men after a dozen years of fighting
against the world, and of being conquered by
their own passions, that is worthy of the name—
worthy of love like Adie's?

She was happy, and that is perhaps enough.
Whether her happiness arose out of her own
purity, and confidence, and faithful generous heart,
or from Laurence Royston, it matters little; the
results were the same, and one could not wish
her, if deluded, less blind, since her delusion
stilled every longing, and filled every hope, and
realized every day-dream.

They sat together on the old stone steps of the
highest terrace, with the clustered green of the
leaves and grapes about and over them—a pretty
picture daintily set. Adie had given up her

mourning dress, and wore instead a mist-tinted,
gossamer-like thing, which draped her gracefully
enough; her glorious hair was wreathed all round
her head in a coronal of thick glossy plaits; and
drooping over her long, colourless neck were some
sprays of scarlet and white blossoms which
Laurence had just fastened there, more with a
view to his own artist-taste than to imperative
fashion. He sat now a step below her, resting
one arm against her knees, and his head on her
shoulder; she was singing to him in her sweet
liquid voice one of those favourite French airs
which she had remembered since a child, and the
tune chimed melodiously in time to the ripple of
the water below the garden-wall. It was something about having a hundred hearts to love with,
and filling them all with one image; a hundred
eyes to gaze upon one face; a hundred tongues
to speak the praise of one, and so forth. Having
reached the third stanza, Adie stopped, and
passing her hand lightly over Laurence's head,
asked if he were asleep, that he was so still.
He looked up in her face with an expression
which betrayed that, if the old serpent Care had

not stolen his way into *her* Eden, he had found *him* out even in her arms. It was but a momentary shade, however, and passed before she could say that it was there.

" Adie, your existence ought to be all sunshine. Tell me how I am to keep the clouds away," said he, idly caressing the hand which had crept into his, like a tame bird to the hand of its feeder. "We cannot be children always; there are red tints amongst the leaves, and some of the flowers look as if blight had breathed upon them; what is coming to us ? "

" Autumn and to-morrow," answered she, with a light laugh; "autumn by the frosted leaves, and to-morrow because to-day is almost gone; I see nothing else. I am glad we came here, it is such a lovely place; and when we go home again, I shall carry it away in my memory, where it will be like a beautiful picture to be looked at whenever I will, by the light of my love."

" Why not stay here always ? " asked Royston, glancing away from his wife; "it is far more pleasant than what you call home. I am not rich, but I have enough to live as we do now,

—enough and to spare. What can you desire more? What a little, restless, dissatisfied heart it is! not content with what she has, she thinks to run to and fro between this paradise and that abode of shades yclept Nevil's Court."

" I must see it again. I am afraid sometimes Grizzie may think I have given up remembering him," said Adie, with a grave air. "I can just see the old room at this minute, where Nicholas used to sit at work, and where I used to thread my needle by the window, until *somebody* came with a dignified step up the stairway. You never ran, Laurence; and now I remember it, you never laugh aloud. How strangely my thoughts run on from one thing to another!—don't they? "

"Yes, Adie, you have some strange conceits. I think you come of a nomade race, for you are erratic in fancy, and if I do not take heed, you will be erratic in body too; you have a taste for wandering, or you would content yourself in this little nest."

"But *Grizzie*, Laurence?" said Adie, in a tone of soft reproach. " Think, if you lay buried in that gloomy old churchyard where the children

11—2

play about, whether you would like me never to come to look at the mound over you. I should feel sad in heaven if I knew *you* had forgotten me. In my grave I think I should know your footfall from others that would pass, and I am sure your very shadow would warm me in my cold bed when it was cast upon it. And Grizzie loved me, Laurence."

" And I love you, Adie."

" Yes ; but it is not the same. I had grieved him ; I can never tell him any more how sorry I am ; but you, I can put my arms about your neck and kiss you,—so, and so,—and you hear me and are pleased. Laurence, I must go back to Nevil's Court."

" Some day, sweetheart, some day ; but not yet."

He put his arm round her, and drew her down to his breast.

" Adie, do you think we shall love each other as well at Eversley ? "

She looked at him in surprise, and asked, " Why should we not ? "

" Because we shall have more difficulties there

than we have here," he made answer. "Here we live for each other—to enjoy our life, to be happy; there, I must work at the old craft, and be careful and watchful. It will seem another world almost."

"Oh, Laurence, we carry our sunshine with us, do we not? We are independent of times and places, being together."

He did not reply, but twitched the leaves unconsciously from a spray which fell over him.

"Why need we care for being poor while we love each other?" Adie went on, caressingly. "I have never been used to luxury until you brought me here. And would *you* never weary for change?"

"Never with you, my darling, never!" said he, with tender earnestness. "Adie, let us keep our summer day as long as it will stay with us. It will be time enough to think of flight when the necessity for change shows itself in our weariness of each other. I shall think you tire of me if you want to get back into the old life so soon."

Adie wondered how Laurence dare breathe

such a suspicion; she did not think she should forgive him, at least not yet; but she added, with a kiss, to show that she was not tired, or tiring, or ever likely to tire, she would give up all thought of going home for the present.

" I wish you would not call Nevil's Court *home*," said Laurence, with a slight tone of annoyance; your home is in my heart."

She promised not to offend again; and the memory of poor Grizzie being set aside once more, Adie returned to her song, and Laurence to his private thoughts. Meantime the sun had gone down; even the red reflection on sea and sky had vanished, and the landscape was over-spread with a solemn tint of gray. With a con-tinuous moan, the south wind came over the waves, which kept up their slow, sad symphony without pause; the vine-leaves stirred and rustled softly till night came down upon them with its dusk silence; darkness there was none, for the moon arose, and the stars shone out upon the skirts of twilight till the day melted imperceptibly into night. And still Adie went on with her song:

" Si j'avais cent cœurs,
  Ils ne seraient remplis que de toi ;
  Si j'avais cent cœurs,
  Aucun d'eux n'aimerait ailleurs."

Laurence rose suddenly, and clasping her in his arms, broke out, in a rich deep voice, into the refrain, which he had learnt from her frequent repetition of it:

" Ma mie,
  Ma douce amie,
  Réponds à mes amours;
  Fidèle
  A cette belle,
  Je l'aimerai toujours."

And with one long farewell look over the wide-spread prospect, they entered the cottage.

X.

PRIVATE SKELETONS.

THE skeleton in Laurence Royston's secret closet was a very grim and ghastly skeleton indeed. It used to track him about the pathways of the cottage-garden, with a hollow menacing footstep. Adie never heard it; but sometimes, through her

pleasant singing and her happy laughter, he was
startled by its tramp at his heels, or the echo of
it coming swiftly from a distance. Then he would
grow almost impatient of her gaiety, as if she
knew what haunted him. Adie wondered, was
silent, and then sad. It would thrust a cold arm
between them, and put them apart; it made a
third at all their meetings, sat at their board, by
their bed, and was as constant to Laurence as his
shadow. He strove hard to be blind and deaf to
its approach; but it was a part of himself,—a
subtle emanation from his evil conscience,—which
he could never part from: his existence was such
as he had made it, with its shadow evermore on
his hearthstone, and the horrible remorse at his
heart. He might forget it for an hour, he might
even defy it for a while, and measure his strength
of mind and will against its torture; but presently
its hour returned, and he was a mere coward,
afraid of the darkness, and trembling at the
rustling of a leaf below his foot.

Adie laughed and sang on; in his moments of
gloom the fondest; when he was grave or stern,
most blithe and cheering. What their life might

have been but for that step in the dark! Sometimes a painful doubt came over the young wife's
mind. Could he be growing weary of her? was
she already losing her power to charm? They
had been a year married, and now another life
hung upon hers; yet sometimes he would leave
her at the cottage with the servant for a week
together, while he made excursions on foot about
the neighbourhood, trying to evade his ghostly
companion by constant movement and change of
place. Yet when he returned to her, how glad
he seemed to stay his weary feet at her side, how
tender, how thoughtful, he could be still! Yes,
he had not ceased to love her.

One day, during a wandering fit, he strayed
into a wood by the wayside, to be out of the glare
of the sun, and lay down on a turfy slope under
the trees. There was an opening before him,
winding away through high arching boughs, and
lost at last in a mist of sunshine. There was no
whisper amongst the branches either of wind or
birds; the very sprays of fern were unstirred.
How weary he was; how dark at heart he must
have been when he saw nothing of the beauty of

these woods; heard nothing but a wail coming up through the trembling air burdened with a pregnant menace to his ears—" I bide my time!" There is not the peace of solitude for such as Laurence Royston in the dim forests; he must up, and go forward again.

Another day he went down to the shore. A flat of dry sand stretched out before him, with the wind sweeping visibly over it; above was a dull sky, boding rain; and to the farthest verge of the horizon lay a turbid, leaden, waveless sea, beaten down from the shore by the strong land-breeze. A dark reef, far out, seemed to glide like a marine monster, as the sullen swell revealed its outline from time to time. There were a few fragments of wood—parts of a wreck, perhaps—scattered near, a solitary bird swooping through the haze, and no other living thing in sight. His limbs were weary, his feet were sore, yet he still kept on, close by the sea, with his face towards it, and his imagination raising threatening shapes out of the mist, while his ears were filled with a wail that outmoaned both wind and tide. For miles on the lonely shore he went, without heeding that the night was gathering around him, and no place in sight were he could claim a shelter;—there was a point in the distance against whose base the waves roared eternally, and high cliffs stretching beyond, reddened with the lurid light of riven storm-clouds;—for miles on the lonely shore, the scene growing wilder as he went forward, hoarse mutterings of thunder in the air, and lurid flashes gleaming athwart the black sea.

Worn out at last, he laid himself down in a hollow of the cliffs, and rested there till dawn; then on again in his abortive flight. Once that day he came in sight of a picturesque and ancient chateau, standing about two hundred paces from the shore. On the side towards the sea, was a planting of young trees, all leaning one way, as if, having bowed to the blasts so often, they were no longer able to raise their heads erect. It was a quaint old place, yet sunny of aspect, with little peaked towers and a great porch, under which were rude stone seats. All about its walls were creeping plants and ivy; in front lay a wide mossy lawn, with a dry fountain, whose brink was matted over with gay flowers, and in the

midst was a broken sundial. Two huge hounds
lay dozing in the sunshine; they were old, worn
out, and toothless, but they lifted up their heads
as the heavy, irregular step of the wayfarer approached; and one rose up, gaunt and grim, and
bounded across the lawn, barking furiously. Did
they scent blood, or was it that Laurence Royston
had the air of a dangerous prowler rather than of
an inoffensive traveller? Cursing between his
teeth, he strode on, so wild and fierce of countenance, that the people whom he met crossed out of
his way. He had become emaciated in body and
feature during his solitary wanderings, and his
expression was such as might have come over the
man's face who played with Satan for his soul,
when, the stake being utterly lost, it was about to
be claimed.

It was evening when he came back to the
cottage, spent with fatigue, and racked by the
poisoned memory he carried in his breast. Adie
was sitting on the steps under the veranda, waiting
and watching for him, as she always did wait and
watch during his absences. The twilight was
closing in; and as autumn drew on, the air had a

more chilling breath, and the wind a more mournful sob. The lonely days of Laurence's absence had dragged over very slowly with his wife; but when she recognized his step upon the roadside, she sprang up, and was away to meet him in an instant, all sense of trouble and neglect dispelled at once. With his arm round her, and her anxious eyes questioning him with their upward look to his, they entered the house. The light inside was nearly gone, so that she could not see the expression of despair that settled down on his face, as they sat hand in hand by the little window which was half shrouded by the rich yellow jasmin and passion-flower that hid the white walls. Yet, if her eyes could not see, her heart felt that all was not well with him; for his fingers were cold, and thrilled often in her clasp. Her idea was, that he must be ill, and, to save her anxiety, trying to conceal his sufferings. She entreated him to tell her what ailed him, and why he was so restless; but he put both questions aside.

"Let us go home to Nevil's Court," suggested Adie, laying her cool hand on his forehead, and speaking very softly.

He started up, and pushed her hand away impatiently, then suddenly snatched it to his lips and kissed it passionately.

" Adie, I will do anything you like, I will go anywhere, but here we will stay no longer; for I am sure there is fever in the air: my brain is like a furnace," he exclaimed.

The tears in Adie's eyes dispersed unfallen. She thanked him so earnestly as to betray how strong her own desire for her old home had been, though she had hidden it from deference to his wishes.

" Home!" she responded, cheerfully; "home! Grizzie, poor old Grizzie! Don't you wish he were there to give us a welcome, Laurence?"

"I do, from my soul, Adie!" he cried, with such fearful energy as to startle her,—"from my soul!"

"The people in the court will be glad, I know," said she, a minute or two after; "Martha and Mrs. Parkes especially. I should like my child to be born there,—I feel as if it ought, Laurence,—then it will be English like you."

The young wife talked on of the future that

was to be so bright and happy to them both in the old haunted house, and laid plans for making it quite a cheerful abode, without displacing any of Grizzie's ancient possessions. "For," she observed, "it seems to me as if he were master there still, and would object to having great changes made. Besides, I like the carved oak chairs and presses—do not you, Laurence?"

He did not seem to hear her prattle, for he made no articulate answer to any of her questions. Perhaps he and his private skeleton were talking together.

XI.

THE PICTURE DREAM.

THEY were back again in Nevil's Court, with Martha, Mrs. Parkes, and the footsteps. On the night of their arrival, the mysterious tramp was heard in the corridor for the first time since Adie's marriage. She listened to it with trembling, recollecting that Grizzie had called it an omen for evil; for she thought of her own hour of trial which was approaching with an indefinable fear, while her heart yearned to Laurence with more than its old passionate love. Was the warning for her, or for both?

One Sabbath afternoon all the house was very hushed; the children were away at church or at school; the doors and windows were all shut, for the air was cold, like the first day of winter. Laurence Royston was in the work-room, graver in hand, and a half-finished plate before him,— he took no note of times and seasons,—as if he intended to distract his thoughts by toil; but instead, he sat waiting,—O God, how anxiously! —as if his own death-sentence hung upon the message he was expecting to hear. They had told him Adie might die; and as the possibility forced itself into his thoughts, he felt almost maddened.

"It cannot be, it shall not be!" he said to himself.

It was not often in his lifetime that this man had prayed; but when that fear came upon him, he besought God slavishly to punish him for his misdeeds in any way but that. So much as he had perilled, so much as he had lost, to possess her, he had a right to keep her. Then he almost defied Heaven to take her from him: she was his by purchase; he had given for her the utmost price that man could pay, and he would not be defrauded of his due. The solitude of the old room, or perhaps Martha's furtive eye, alone witnessed these ravings, which seemed to shadow forth some hidden deed. Possibly, that deed it was that kindled his pale eye with lurid fire, and haunted him with its presence always. There were great drops on his forehead, which he wiped away with a trembling hand, while his mouth worked violently. This agony of suspense was insufferable, and what long, long hours it lasted! He dared not go to his darling, lest the blackness of his curse, overshadowing, should destroy her; and yet, when the night fell, no one had come to tell him whether he was the father of a living child or the husband of a dead wife. The darkness crept on unawares as he waited and listened; at last he lighted the lamp and tried to read, but there was neither sense nor continuity in the page, and he soon threw it aside.

Utterly exhausted in mind and body, a sort of lethargic trance fell upon him, and with that a fearful dream. At first he seemed to be driven onward violently over a dark, heaving gulf, and then hurled down the yawning vortex into a darkness that might be felt. Presently, through this darkness moved vivid, shapeless lights, which seemed to portend the advent of some nameless horror. He tried to draw himself away, he struggled to cover his face, for he *felt* what was coming; but his efforts were as the efforts of a prisoner chained hand and foot and powerless to stir. Then he nerved himself to look, and the old room in Nevil's Court—where he was sitting—appeared in his dream. It was all a-glow, as with the ruddy heat of a Yule-tide fire, and old Nicholas Drew was there. Then was enacted before his sight the whole scene of the murder, even to the dropping of the glove. That incident startled and awoke him.

" Where is that glove? who found it? who has it now?" he asked himself, fearfully. All the vision had resolved itself into the lost glove; he could think of nothing but that. "The other was burnt; *it* must have been destroyed too; I heard no mention of a glove having been found." He glanced suspiciously round the room, shrinking down into his chair in the very attitude of guilty fear; whilst his skeleton at his elbow kept whispering, " Where is the *glove?* Who has the *glove?* Whoever has the *glove* has your life with it ! "

How long it was from the passing of the vision to the entrance of Martha he could never tell; it might have been five minutes, and it might have been a night-time: but he was himself again the moment the woman spoke.

" My mistress has asked for you, sir," she said, briefly; not a syllable of warning or congratulation.

He asked if the child lived, and was answered that it did, with the same coldness. Even at that moment a suspicion had time to enter into his mind. " That woman has found the glove, and she is watching me," he thought: but he passed her with an air of over-acted carelessness, and went to Adie's room. Mrs. Parkes made a spasmodic effort to utter the proper felicitations, and failed

with a choking sob. He did not heed her, but
looked in between the closed curtains of the bed,
to meet a wan, wistful smile on Adie's face.

" Oh, Laurence, I am so happy, because of the
boy," she whispered, as he bent over her. " Look
at him: they say he is like me;" and her eyes
lighted up with the fun of the idea, that such a
queer little mortal could resemble anything but a
bundle of soft muslin and fine flannel, with a
doll's feeble face.

Laurence hid his feelings under an appearance
of exuberant joy. He could not be really glad;
for the boy was born under his curse, and he
remembered at the moment those terrible words:
" I will visit the sins of the fathers upon the
children." He was in haste for once to leave her,
and steal back to his haunted solitude; and perhaps Adie was glad that he should go; for she
wanted to have her baby to herself, to think about
it, to whisper to it, and to pray for it.

It was not long before the young mother was
about again, brightening the dim old rooms with
her cheerful face. Laurence liked to hear her
crooning nursery-songs with the child in her

lap, to see her play with it on the floor, or dance it in her arms. But when she had soothed it to sleep on her bosom, and laid it down in its cradle, he fancied that his skeleton] kept watch by it, and shadowed the boy's face with deadly wings; he was never easy until she took it again to her heart, for he thought it safer there, as well he might, in the sanctuary of a pure mother's love. It was not strong; and by-and-by there came a look of angel beauty on the tiny features—a soft radiance, as if a smile from Heaven had shone upon them, and left His trace and mark that the great Reaper might know it when he came that way. Adie had her thoughts and fears, but she kept them secret in her own mind, and tended the child with a reverent and most tender watchfulness. She liked to deck it gaily, and to work for it; she made advanced garments of ingenious device, as if she were thus pledging him to stay with her; and all the while that he seemed to be fading away, her prayer to God was, that she might keep him.

Laurence used to sit by the second window—not in Nicholas Drew's old place—working at

his craft assiduously; while Adie, within range
of his sight, sewed or nursed the child, and sang,
now in a plaintive, now in a gay tone, the old
ballads.

Meantime winter advanced. In the Minster
yard the poplars were despoiled of their foliage,
and in the Bishop's garden lay the dead leaves
whirled into sodden heaps, while the trees looked
black and naked against the walls. The first day
that the snow fell was a notable one to Adie.
It was early in December, and the merry shouts
of children down in the court called her from
the fireside to see the broad white flakes fluttering
earthward. The little child stretched his hands
upwards and laughed; the sound did her heart
good to hear. She danced him on her hand, and
prattled to him gleefully, until their rather noisy
mirth caused Laurence to lift his eyes from his
work to watch them. The two were so much
occupied with each other, that he enlisted none
of their attention, and with a half-sigh he arose,
and went across the room to the hearth.

Standing before the fire, thoughtful and moody,
the same trance-like feeling came over him as

he had experienced on the night of his child's birth, and again the vision of the murder and the lost glove enacted itself before his fancy. His face grew absolutely livid, and his eyes opened with a wild, affrighted stare.

At this instant Adie turned round and caught his awful expression; she had time to decipher it indeed, for so startled was she, that for a moment she never spoke, and Laurence did not know himself observed.

" Oh, Laurence, Laurence, what is it?" she exclaimed, at last, going to where he stood. " Why do you look so? you seem quite affrighted."

He tried to laugh, but it was a ghastly effort. He said it was a spasm of pain at his heart, but that it would soon pass.

" Laurence, let us leave this place," she said, looking all round the room; "it is not good for us to be here. I feel as if it were haunted with something worse than the footsteps. Baby does not thrive, and you often appear ill, and I shudder to be left alone. I am satisfied now, for I am sure dear old Grizzie would not like us to stay if he knew how we suffer. Shall we go back to that pretty cottage by the seaside? It was very happy being there, Laurence."

"So it was, Adie. You might be happy any-where, with your good, simple, loving heart; but not so can I; I must have more life and stir; my thoughts stagnate often till they breed frightful fancies. Let us go to London."

"So be it. After baby is christened we will go. St. Barbe and kind old Mrs. Parkes would be disappointed if we went before."

And thus it was finally agreed upon.

XII.

NEMESIS.

It had been a day of great preparation with Martha and Mrs. Parkes, for Adie had asked St. Barbe and Marsh the printseller, who stood godfathers for the child, to spend the evening in Nevil's Court; and the unusual festivity could not be signalized without much needless trouble.

A dance had even been hinted at, but promptly negatived by Laurence, who said briefly that such a thing was not to be thought of—and, besides, they had no friends. This was one of his strange, incomprehensible ideas, that they had no friends ; whereas Adie's former schoolfellows had come often to see her and the baby, and would have gladly renewed their old acquaintance, if he had not been so cold and distant, that the most sociably disposed were soon discouraged in their attempts to know them. Even St. Barbe rarely saw the inside of their door, and had never broken bread with them since the death of Nicholas Drew; the same with Curll also, though he had done Royston several kind offices since he had returned to live at Eversley. Martha did her share of work with a stolid, unsympathizing indifference; but Mrs. Parkes, who had undertaken to cook a supper worthy of the time—for it was Christmas—made noise and stir enough to have spoilt a dozen turkeys instead of roasting one. Then all her talk was redolent of sugar, and spice, and lemons, and strong waters; for the worthy woman's appreciation of the good things of this life was in the ratio of her scant enjoyment of them.

Adie made Laurence put on his wedding-suit; and she herself donned a delicate-tinted silk taffety, brocaded with bright flowers, which had been the Frenchman's bridal gift to her; matron-wise, she would cover her luxuriant black hair with a piece of cobweb-lace, which came to a peak on the forehead, and hung down in two broad lappets behind. The excitement and plea-sure of the day had brought a deeper, softer lustre to her large eyes, and the vermeil flush on her cheek was as pure and fresh as in her maiden prime. The child, too, was decked in rich Indian muslin, all finely embroidered, with gay sash and shoulder-knots of blue, which con-trasted well with the velvet-softness and purity of his little dimpled arms and shoulders. The women of the court had one and all been up to admire him, somewhat to the discomfiture of Laurence, who at length retreated into the closet, and left them to exhaust their superlatives of admiration unrestrained.

They were all clustered upon the hearth, talking in chorus, the boy being in his mother's arms, surveying the whole proceedings with an air of princely satisfaction, when Martha entered from the corridor with a short comely dame in black, who joined the group, and added her meed of praise. Adie was holding the boy aloft when this person came in; but she instantly took him down, and let him hide her face against her neck, for it was not considered a good omen that the nurse who went from house to house to lay out corpses for burial should show herself at a christening. Mrs. Parkes made a loud exclamation and said that Judith ought to have known better, and Martha too.

" I did not know any one could object," said the nurse, in a meek voice; " I don't believe much in fancies myself. The bonnie bairn will thrive none the worse for Judith's blessing, I'm sure."

Mrs. Parkes turned an indignant shoulder upon her, and, thus repudiated, the poor soul, whose vocation made her everywhere an unwelcome guest, drew back and spoke to Martha, who, with icy face and folded hands, stood looking on.

Presently the two were observed to whisper together, while Judith glanced mysteriously at the
rich lace on Adie's head. Mrs. Parkes insisted
on her remarks being uttered aloud.

"We are all women, and all friends; there
is no secrets," said she, moved, perhaps, as much
by past indignation as present curiosity.

Judith hesitated, and Martha went out.

"What is it, nurse? tell us," asked Adie, in
her pleasant voice. "You are not amongst
mourners to-day, and may therefore speak aloud."

"We were only saying that it was a pity you
had chose that lace for your cap," answered the
little woman, growing red and uneasy.

"And why, pray?" snapped Mrs. Parkes.
"It is as beautiful a piece of old point as was
ever seen in Nevil's Court, and is worth its weight
in gold a score of times over. Why shouldn't
it be worn if Adie likes? nothing could look so
good or so well on her black hair."

"Maybe," responded the nurse; "it was only
because I cut off a piece of it to cover Nicholas
Drew's face when I streaked him for his coffin."

"Lord save us!" gasped Mrs. Parkes, dismayed

at the result of her abrupt curiosity; for Adie's face faded to a deathly pallor, and she sank down into a chair. One of the women poured out a little of the wine which stood on the table, that they might drink the boy's health, and put it to her lips. She swallowed a few drops, and recovered herself quickly, smiling to cover her pain.

This incident dispersed the gossips; they hastily emptied their glasses, and went out together, leaving only Mrs. Parkes.

"You must not heed anything that silly old Judith says," observed the worthy woman, in a cheering tone; "she is brimful of cranky notions, each one more crazed than the other. Don't think of pulling off that pretty lace, for it becomes you beautiful."

"No; if an evil omen it is, the warning is given," answered Adie, softly. "I shall be so glad to go away from this old haunted house; it is like a constant nightmare upon our spirits."

"Yet you have done a deal to make it lightsome," said Mrs. Parkes. "That nice picture

over the fireplace, and Martha has polished up
the panels till every one shines like a looking-
glass. We shall be sorry to lose you; and I
doubt whether anybody else will care to come.
You see, the house has got a bad name."

Adie made no reply; and Mrs. Parkes, having
culinary anxieties on her mind, went out, pur-
posing to ease her annoyance by lecturing the
obnoxious Martha on her imprudence.

When she was gone, Adie sought Laurence in
the closet, where he had chosen to shut himself
up. He was leaning against the dingy window,
looking out into the Bishop's garden, where the
early twilight of December was fast replacing its
frosty sunshine. At the sound of his wife's step,
he turned; and as she came beside him he put
his arm round her fondly.

" I suppose your little heart is satisfied now the
gossips have flattered Laury," he said. "You
could do very well without me."

She looked up wistfully in his face, not under-
standing him, yet not liking to question, for his
manner of late had been strange in the extreme.
He was tender by fits and starts; and he had

asked her more than once before if she should grieve were he gone.

"Adie, you see that high wall at the farther side of the garden," he abruptly remarked, after a minute's silence; "what is at the other side of it—streets or fields?"

"A steep bank first, and then a row of houses, called Bishop's Lane: you know it very well."

"Yes, I remember it;—and beyond the houses is the River Ness and the open country? I know those fields; we have walked there."

"Often,—we passed St. Mark's Church. How cold it is here, Laurence; baby shivers: let us go to the fireside."

She drew him out of the gloomy little den into the broad light of the outer room, and made him sit down on the long settle beside her.

"Now, Laurence, admire our handiwork," she began, with an effort of sprightliness. "I don't believe you would ever see anything if I did not order you. There is my picture over the fire, all framed about with holly and scarlet berries. Look, too, how Martha has polished the panels of the press, and even of the wainscot. We wear quite a festive air."

"Yes,"—he glanced round slightly, seeing in those bright dark panels so many repetitions of his phantom pictures,—"yes, Adie, you would make sunshine everywhere but in a diseased mind. I wonder often why certain circumstances are permitted,—why, for instance, you, sweetheart, as fresh, innocent, and guileless as our child in your arms, should have been suffered to link your fate with mine,—why you should have loved me."

"I can answer your last speculation—why I should have loved you—because I could not help it," answered Adie, with a pouting smile. "It was sorely against my will, as you very well know."

"I have tried to make you happy,—you *have* been happy, Adie."

"To my heart's desire, Laurence, I only want to see you wear your old careless way, and to hear you talk to me as you used to do, and my measure of joy would be full: but perhaps it would be too much at once."

" Every night, Adie, I see you on your knees,—
do you ever pray for me?"

" I try always; but it seems as if,—shall I say
it, Laurence?"

" Yes, my darling, speak on."

" Well, it seems as if I were put away out of
God's hearing when I pray for you. It is not
that my words are cold, or that my heart is
not in them, but as if mercy had covered its face.
I have wept sometimes, Laurence, I was so sad
for you."

" Don't waste your tears, Adie; there ought
to be cleansing power in them; but if your
prayers are to a deaf ear, they will be useless.
I wish, for your sake and the lad's, I were a
better man."

"Laurence, you know what is promised to
those who sincerely repent."

" But I do *not* repent. I only curse my evil
fate. Do you remember likening me to a figure
in a certain picture?"

" Oh, yes; how wrong it was of me! I was
quite ashamed that you should know. I hoped
you had forgotten it."

"No, sweetheart, I have never forgotten one word of yours; and the similitude there was striking."

"It was a foolish thought of mine; I have never seen the resemblance since; so it must have been a mere passing expression."

"Your loving fancy has idealized me out of all nature, Adie; you do not see my faults, or else you are fond of them for their owner's sake."

"Do not be so sure, Laurence; you want mending in many ways, and I think of setting seriously to work to mend you."

"That task will need a more cunning hand than this, sweetheart," said he, taking her slender fingers in his: "I think if the jarred, flawed, leaking vessel were all broken up, it would be best; it is not safe to stow your happiness away in it."

"Laurence, you make me very sad when you talk in that fashion; I do not understand you. You know that if I were without you, I and baby might as well be lying in St. Mark's churchyard by poor old Grizzie; we should not care to live by ourselves."

"I do believe you love me with all my sins on my head."

"Doubt anything but my love, Laurence; for I can forgive you everything but such a doubt."

They stayed there by the fireside for a long time, talking of things to them important, but to others trivial, until Martha came in to put more logs on the fire, to close the shutters, and light the lamp. Her master was gayer than usual; Adie's voice had charmed him to a better mood; and the woman, in her furtive, watchful way, took note of it. They became silent when she entered; and as her listed step seemed always to deepen instead of breaking the hush, the noise of a rising wind outside resounded mournfully through the court. It drove sharp, rattling gusts of hail and sleet noisily against the windows, then lulled and rose again to fury. Martha said it was going to blow a hurricane, as she fastened the windows.

"Let it blow; we are under warm shelter," responded Laurence, carelessly.

"Ay, master, and them who have to bide it out of doors may bide it easily enough, if they have clean consciences," said Martha, significantly.

He turned round to the fire, with a dark, wrathful look on his face. Adie, who was singing to the child, had not heard this brief colloquy. At that moment voices below were heard, steps ascended the stairway, and Marsh and St. Barbe appeared at the door.

It was a rather oddly assorted company which sat round that Christmas supper-table. Laurence Royston and Adie, the courteous, coldly-polished old Frenchman, and the rough Marsh, and finally, the round, rubicund, and honest Mrs. Parkes. Martha glided about, with a cat-like velvety step, serving them, always at hand, but never obtrusive —a model of a waiting-woman, with a face as blank as a shadow. The cold being carefully shut out, the old room looked and felt cosy enough; and when Marsh had thawed into good-humour, he ceased to remember his chilly walk out of the Barbican. The Frenchman also seemed in a state of ineffable beatitude, as indeed he always was, with good cheer before him. These two and Mrs. Parkes had the talk for some time to themselves; for Laurence was very silent, and Adie was disturbed to see him so depressed. By-and-by, however, he shook off the fit, and laughed with the rest, which his wife seeing, she also became at ease. Mrs. Parkes had the satisfaction of seeing her culinary labours duly appreciated and duly honoured, so that, when the Christmas bowl was set on the table, with all the accessories for the compounding of a drink which St. Barbe called *ponche divin*, it needed but that to raise her spirits to their utmost height. At any other time she might have been considered as too exuberantly gay. Marsh was to compound the bowl; and that being done, the health of young Laury was drunk,—by St. Barbe sentimentally, by the printseller enjoyingly, and by Mrs. Parkes tearfully. Perhaps Adie put up a brief prayer as her lips touched the glass; and Laurence, without tasting, and almost unconsciously, set his down again.

"You do not drink, my friend Laurence," remarked the Frenchman, gaily. "You must drink to your son—you must."

With a nervous hand Royston lifted his glass

and drained it: when he set it down again, it
rang on the table with the tremor of his grasp;
but soon his cold, pale, blue eyes lit up, and a
red spot of excitement burnt on each hollow
cheek.

It now became evident that Marsh meditated
making a speech, for he became restless and
flurried, half rose from his seat, ruffled his scanty
grey hair, and, with a hem, began. He hoped
there were none present who had forgotten the
former master of that house; he had not: he
missed him daily. They were friends; they had
been boys and men together, and friends always.
He had loved Nicholas Drew for his virtues, and
revered him for his genius; nobody had known
him better, or appreciated him more highly. They
anticipated what he had to say: this good old
man lay in his grave unavenged. The toast he
had to propose was, " A speedy capture and short
shrift to his murderer."

During this exordium, Martha had been standing opposite her master, with her eyes looking at
him from beneath the half-downcast lids, and in
her hand a glass which he had handed to her to

drink his son's health. As it was finished she
lifted it to her lips and drained it, still watching
him. Adie hesitated a moment, then swallowed
a few drops, while her husband drank the contents of his glass hastily, and cried, with a sort
of defiance in his tone,—

"To that I say, Amen."

A few seconds of silence ensued, during
which Martha glided to and fro, putting a few
matters within reach previously to leaving the
room.

"Let us have a game at cards," suggested
Laurence, hastily. "You like cards, St. Barbe?
all Frenchmen have a taint of the gambler."

The clockmaker agreed; and Marsh said that
it was years since he had touched anything of
the kind, but he would join in. Adie did not
like this; but there was an eager, restless excitement in her husband's manner, that she did not
care to thwart. He asked her to find some cards.
She replied at first that there were none in the
house; then suddenly recollected that there was
a very old pack, which had belonged to Nicholas,
in her box where she stored her treasures;

Martha had not yet gone out, and she bade her
fetch the little chest from her chamber.

"The cards, mistress,—must I get them out?"
asked she, quietly.

"No; you can bring the box here," was the
reply.

The woman returned in a minute, saying it
was too heavy to lift; but if Adie would give her
the key, she could find what she wanted. With
an ejaculation of impatience, Laurence started up,
and fetched the box 'himself. It was of trifling
size, and Mrs. Parkes suggested that Martha was
good for nothing, if that were too much for her.
The cards were produced, and the three men were
soon earnestly engaged in their game. Adie and
Mrs. Parkes sat on the long settle by the fire,
talking, while the former carelessly turned over
the contents of the box. Her fingers came in
contact with the dead white rose, which she lifted
out and smiled over thoughtfully.

Martha came up to her.

"Shall I put the box away, mistress?" she
asked, preparing to lift it up.

"No, leave it," said Adie; and taking another

thing from it, she tripped behind Laurence Royston's chair, and laying one hand softly on his shoulder, dropped the other before him, asking, in a whisper, " Do you know that glove, Laurence ? "

He recognized it instantaneously, and started up from his chair with a terrible oath; his face was livid, his eye was murderous.

" I never saw it in my life before! Why do you come to me with such fool's questions?" he exclaimed. Then reading the startled surprise in the faces all around him, he added, " What is the glove to me? what should I know about it? take it away, Adie! "

He flung it over towards the fire, but it fell short upon the hearth, and was picked up by Mrs. Parkes, who examined it carefully. From the first moment of his outbreak, Adie never took her eyes from her husband's face; they dilated first with a pained astonishment, then darkened with a wavering mist,—a dull, speechless agony. She had penetrated the mask which he strove vainly to retain upon his traitor countenance. Marsh laid on his host's shoulder

a heavy grasp, and St. Barbe, passing round
to the farther side of him, whispered low in
his ear a few emphatic words. Royston's eyes
flickered from one to the other, and then settled
on Adie.

"You have killed me with your silly love!"
said he, in a kind of mad rage; thus blindly
changing the suspicion which had flashed across
the minds of the two men into a dark certainty
that he was Nicholas Drew's murderer.

They were the last words that for many months
struck the soul of the poor Flower of Nevil's
Court. A shrill, passionate cry broke from her,
which echoed and re-echoed through the haunted
house; then she seemed to stiffen into a statue;
all expression passed from her features; all speculation from her eyes; her hands fell as if volition
were utterly gone from her, and without one
word or one gesture, without even turning her
head to follow their movements, she let the
Christmas guests depart, taking her husband
with them. As he went out, Laurence looked
back at her with a wild, remorseful pity.
Had he not done her wrong enough that his

last words to her should be that cruel, cruel reproach?

Once out in the court, self-preservation, man's strongest instinct in most cases, prompted Laurence Royston to make one desperate effort to escape. The two men who had been his guests had loosed their grasp to let him pass down the outer stairs; and rushing to the archway, he, favoured by the darkness, contrived to elude their pursuit, and to disappear in one of the numerous narrow lanes abutting on Friargate. Thence to the open country, under cover of night, he made his way; and though a hue and cry was raised after him, he was supposed to have effected his escape from the kingdom, as he was never traced.

Poor Adie remained long in her unconscious state, blank and unimpressible as a bronze image. Martha watched and tended her and the boy with unremitting care and fondness, striving by many a little art to awaken her senses. She liked to sit in the open air, especially when the sun shone, gazing pitifully at heaven, and pulling to pieces flowers that people brought her

from the fields; but she never took any notice
either of her boy or Martha, or of any other
person whom Christian charity impelled to visit
her.   She was regarded as one on whom
God's chastening hand had been laid with signal
heaviness; but still as one who suffered for
another's sin.

When the dark days began to come round
again, in the long stormy October and clouded
November nights, there might occasionally be
seen the figure of a man slinking along from
shadow to shadow under the Minster walls, until
he came into Nevil's Court. If all was still, he
would hide in the archway, and listen for any
one coming or going to and fro in the house;
and sometimes he gathered courage stealthily to
mount the old wooden stair, and peep in through
the uncurtained window at poor Adie, sitting
like a dark statue by the fire, Laury playing
on the hearth, and Martha busy at the work
with which she helped to maintain them. After
a few minutes of this stealthy watch, he would

glide away as noiselessly as he had come; and not seldom he would lie crouching like a miserable, homeless dog in a corner of the court until the window was dark, and all the city was a-bed. His appearance grew more and more haggard and awful; and at last his strength was so spent, that any one meeting him might have thought it was Laurence Royston's ghost, but not that unhappy man in the flesh. One keen, stinging night he had trailed his steps to the archway, and there he fell, utterly spent with hunger, fatigue, and misery. After lying for a few minutes thus, he staggered to his feet, to make an effort to see Adie once more, and climbed the stair clinging to the rail. Adie only was there; neither the child nor Martha; so he opened the door and went in, crying, "Adie, I am dying; let me die here!" and staggering across the floor, he fell at her feet, clinging feebly to her knees. At the sound of his voice she started up, looked at him eagerly, and sinking beside him, she drew his head upon her breast, saying, with a pitiful, yearning love, "*Here*, Laurence, here!" Martha came in, and regarded

the scene with amazement.   Adie bid her shut
to the door.

"Say a prayer, Adie; God will hear you,"
gasped the dying man; and before the words
were done he had gone to his account.

———————————

This event, startling and painful as it was,
restored Adie to her right mind. At first she
was questioning continually, "Is *he* forgiven?
Did God hear my prayer?" But at length she
was still, and left her cause in His faithful hands.
She lived long, patient, gentle, full of good and
charitable offices.   The poor knew her; those
who were sick and in misery knew her, and
blessed her name; in the old long ago she would
have been canonized as a saint; if ever suffering
purified humanity to saintly holiness, Adie was
thus purified.   Laury lived to return her love,
and to be a man of mark in his day and generation; but he and the Flower of Nevil's Court,
and all the other personages named in this story,
have been churchyard dust these many, many
years; though the tale still goes, that in the

dead of the Christmas night a wild, piercing cry frightens out of the silence a host of mournful, wailing echoes, and that the tramp of the footsteps in the corridor is to be heard whenever calamity is coming to any of those who dwell in the Haunted House.

From the Diary.

———•◇•———

BELLE had a little fault to find with my story of
The Haunted House when we came to the end of it.
She wanted to know if it were not as easy to write
pleasant things as dismal things. I could have
told her that it was not as easy to me when I
wrote that. Hearing these ancient lucubrations
of mine carries me back to the mournful Eversley
days, when there seemed so little likelihood of
my life ever realizing what it is to be truly
satisfied.

" Why did you not make the people get married
and live happily ever afterwards, like you and
papa ? " says she.

" My dear, how do you know what probation
your papa and I went through before we attained
to our present condition ? " returned I.

"I suppose you had your *crosses*, as Hannah observes, but I don't like people being murdered and going mad in books—why should they?" demanded Miss Unreasonable. "I cannot drink my tea for thinking of that poor Adie! No, mamie, indeed you are not going away just as you have made us all miserable! You must sit down again, and hear Miss Mostyn tell how she went to Madame Freschon's; that will be fun, I know! I like stories about school, and she has promised to tell me it for ever so long past—have you not, Mossy?"

Miss Mostyn owned the impeachment, and then gave us the following account of how she went to school in France when she was a girl.

MADAME FRESCHON'S.

In the foggy, gray dawn of a January morning, some dozen years ago, I, then a mite of a girl aged thirteen, was left on the deck of the *City of Glasgow* steamer, lying below London Bridge, for the purpose of transportation to school on the other side of the Channel. It was bitter cold, and my cousin Jack, who had come with me in a cab from Islington, had given me a bashful kiss and gone home again; assuring me that I should be quite safe and that nobody would touch me; but that, as it did not appear clear when we should get off, it was not of any use for him to wait to see me start. I was not sorry when he disappeared in the fog, for cousin Jack always laughed at me, and made me feel shy; because

though he was a great, lumbering, awkward
fellow, he was clever, and made fun of everybody
—even of uncle Sampson and aunt Martha, who
were good people.

When he was quite gone, I deposited myself
on a bench with my feet a good quarter of a yard
from the deck, and sat holding my little cloak
very tight, while my little nose grew ominously
red with stoically repressed tears. Beyond the
vessel it was impossible to see five yards in any
direction, so that I was free to fancy all sorts of
dangers assailing me on my perch. The first
came in the shape of a man with a mop and
pail to wash the deck, who invited me to go
below, which I declined doing on the plea that
I preferred to remain where I was: this assertion
of my new-born independence helped me to
swallow down my rising tears, and to look my
position in the face. The position aforesaid was,
for the present, a damp one, but I endured it
with equanimity, and, having tucked my feet
farther out of the way, I speculated on the probability of seeing home again; so dense a wall of
mist was built up between me and the shore. It

seemed almost a lifetime ago since I had choked over my cup of coffee, and aunt Martha, in her nightcap, had patted me on the back, in the little parlour at Islington, to help it down. My philosophy could not have been steady much longer under these sorrowful reminiscences, when fortunately there came diversion for my thoughts in the shape of a large Newfoundland dog. A noble fellow he was—tall, and with a feathery black tail, and curls all over him, and beautiful beseeching brown eyes, full of intelligence and generosity. He first paid his respects to the man with the mop, and then trotted up to me in a friendly and cordial manner which opened my heart to him at once. I asked him what his name was; an inquiry which he received as an overture towards a more intimate acquaintance, and which he answered by sniffing at my little basket, wherein lay a parcel of delicate sandwiches, intended to sustain me during the voyage. He rose majestically, planted one paw on my lap, and flourished his majestic tail, which I thought so nice of him that I instantly opened my store, intending to regale him with one of those dainty parallelograms of bread and ham, as a reward for his pretty behaviour.

I suppose his appetite must have been keen that morning, for I am sure he was an honest dog; but somehow, in his haste to thank me, he knocked the parcel out of my hand upon the wet deck, and while I said, pathetically, "Oh, naughty dog! how could you do so?" he quietly munched up every sandwich, and then deliberately asked for more. I showed him the empty paper and shook my head, and suffered him to put his nose into the basket, whence he withdrew it with a plaintive expression of disappointment and regret, in which it was impossible not to sympathise. He then sat down beside me and listened, while I drew a touching picture of the extremities to which I might possibly be reduced by his conduct; "I may even have to eat my boots," I was saying, when a loud laugh close behind me, which the wren at the top of St. Paul's might have heard, caused me nearly to tumble off my perch. It was the captain, into whose care cousin Jack had consigned me; a great rubicund man, and the master of the thief.

The paper, rolled up into a baton, with which I was mildly enforcing my argument on the dog's mind, told the story of my loss.

"Never mind, little one, you shall have your breakfast with me," he said, kindly.

Other passengers began to arrive with luggage, cloaks, cross voices, and confusion, and there was so much to watch that was novel and amusing, that I forgot how dreary I ought to feel. Amongst others came two girls, who made it known to me that they were returning to the same school as myself, having been spending their Christmas at home, in Norfolk. They were sunk in the depths of grief; which continued some time, harrowing my young mind with doleful predictions of what we should all have to go through when we arrived at Madame Freschon's. We exchanged a few confidences and were mutually pleased, when the vessel at last began to move; upon which my future companions hastily disappeared into the cabin.

It was a doleful voyage; fog above and fog below, and fog all round; nothing to be seen anywhere but cold, gray, steamy fog! More than once the captain exhorted me to go below; but, finding me obstinate and immovable, he at last let me alone; but the stewardess—of whose amenity of disposition the less said the better—forcibly took me off by one arm, and made me feel myself a prisoner of the state-cabin. Having got me there, she made me drink coffee and eat biscuits; but was invincible on the subject of oranges, for which I petitioned.

The Misses Jones, my schoolfellows that were to be, had hidden themselves in berths at the top, where they lay, groaning miserably; and the only occupants of the cabin, besides myself, were a tall, strong woman, who had not yet loosened hold of her umbrella, and a little boy of about eight years old, whose vivacity she seemed bent on crushing in the bud.

I know not how the rest of the voyage was got over, but I remember feeling myself once more on land on very unsteady limbs, and in a misanthropic frame of mind. An old gentleman and a younger one took undisputed possession of Miss Jones, her sister, and myself, and handed us over to the Custom-house authorities, in such a state of

mental and physical prostration that my tongue
lifted up no remonstrance when my basket was
opened by an individual with mustachios, and
myself undressed by a little woman in black, with
froggy hands. The world was a cheat and
happiness a fraud, and I had found it out. Oh,
that I had been born a boy!

We were next transferred to an inn, where we
were shut up for two hours in a room with dark
blue walls, and a picture of Napoleon scaling
the Alps. Those two hours were very long, but
they came to an end at last. The old gentleman,
who was Madame Freschon's father, and the
young one, who was Monsieur Emile, her brother,
reappeared in a yellow voiture, not unlike a
tilted cart. Into this vehicle we were bestowed;
the Joneses sitting in the seat behind, and I in
front, where I could look out. We started at a
foot's pace, leaving the two gentlemen to follow
with the baggage, I suppose. The driver was
very silent until we got out of Calais, but then
he began to whistle, and occasionally broke into
a stave, each verse of which ended with "*La
liberté ou la mort!*" As night was falling, and

a thick fog still reigned, my vision of this new country was limited. I only made out that the road we travelled ran by the side of the canal, and that, on the other side, it was bordered by stunted willows.

We had been creeping on for upwards of an hour and a half at the very slowest of snail's gallops, when, at a bend in the road, I perceived that we were approaching a town. The willows gave place to cottages, from the low, uncurtained windows of which fire-light streamed across the road. The elder Miss Jones immediately gave signs of becoming hysterical; and, when we entered a narrow street dimly illuminated by little oil lamps, her sobs, mingled with vituperative expressions against the place, the people, and things in general, became really quite alarming. I endeavoured to insinuate a bit of comfort by saying, "Never mind," and then asking the younger sister what was the matter? "Oh, she is always so; she can't help it," was the reply. When I was speculating on the unhappy state of a girl wailing incessantly—like an Irish widow at a wake—the voiture entered the market-place,.

where chaffering was going on in a noisy and
confusing way. Thence we passed into another
narrow street, turned a sharp angle, and stopped
before some great wooden gates set in a high
wall. The driver descended and opened those
ominous portals; my heart beat like a hammer;
Miss Jones moderated her lament, and the voiture
passed into a large court-yard where the ghostly
shadows of some great trees were dimly discern-
ible waving against a background of masonry.

"Here is the old den, Minnie; be quiet,
do!" said the younger Miss Jones, in an emphatic
whisper.

The house-door was opened; and, dazed by
the sudden burst of light from within, for a
minute or two I could see nothing but a crowd
of girls clustered like bees on the staircase. I
was lifted from the voiture and set on my feet
in the hall by a stout female servant; for, though
lively, I was stiff with cold. The Joneses
followed, and we were ushered into a brick-
floored parlour by a plain-featured, light-haired
woman—the English teacher. Here, in state, sat
Madame Freschon, in a Cashmere wrapper with

a lace bonnet-de-nuit on her head, and over that a cambric handkerchief. She had just woke up from a nap, and looked as dignified as it was possible for a little, stout lady to look under any circumstance. I thought her very comfortable and kind in manner. She kissed us all on both sides of our faces, chatted in French with the Joneses, and then dismissed them to their companions; me, as a stranger, she detained to ask questions, in broken English, and to give me a little encouragement. I had some coffee with her; then she rang her bell twice, a summons which brought Mademoiselle Laure, a sort of half-boarder, into the presence. To her care madame consigned me, having first repeated the double kiss, and wished me "a good rest."

Mademoiselle Laure was a taciturn person, who carried a key to unlock a certain green gate which cut off communication between the second and third stories of the house. She led me up a wide staircase and passed some doors whence issued a hum of girls; then up again, until we reached a great room containing eight beds, separated into compartments with little white curtains. Across this room were two stands of basins, and from the roof depended a lamp, which my conductress lighted. She then guided me into one of the compartments, unlooped the curtains; and, notifying that I must manage as I could for nightclothes—as our boxes had not come—left me in privacy. Everything was white and exquisitely clean, from the boards of the floor to the wainscot which rose on three sides of the bed to within a couple of yards of the ceiling. I rather liked the aspect of things in general; but, oh! how hard the mattress was. I ascertained afterwards that it was stuffed with straw. Madame considers straw mattresses wholesome; I daresay they are, for I remember no inconvenience after the first night.

I was in that state of active wakefulness when every sense is alert. The distant buzz of voices, the occasional clapping of doors, and at last a rush—a scutter—a scamper of hundreds of feet up the stairs. The girls were coming to bed. One torrent poured into the dortoir—more poured off in all directions. A silence fell as the great door was shut, and a voice cried out for order.

In a minute, appeared in my division a girl who talked to herself in whispers—she was repeating a lesson; she undressed and laid down beside me, first taking the kindly precaution to cover me up well. In five minutes the lamp was extinguished, and a quarter of an hour after, all the dortoir seemed asleep, but myself.

A noisy bell awoke us at five to the dim, cold, lamp-light again, and everybody turned out in an instant; I with the rest, bent for the present on exercising my imitative faculty, and doing what I saw others do. At six the bell rang again, and all rushed downstairs—along the corridor— out at a glass-door—across a little court, and into a detached building which was the classe. There were between seventy and eighty girls, chiefly French, but with a sprinkling of English. These were divided into three classes, each of which occupied one of the rooms into which the building was divided by sliding-doors. There were cold, comfortless-looking stoves in the centre of each; an estrade for the teacher at the upper end, and down either side benches fixed to the walls, with desks divided by panels at each seat, a box for books overhead, and a narrow ledge fastened to the floor, on which to rest the feet. When seated in these boxes or stalls, we could not overlook each other without rising, which was forbidden under a penalty. Every girl's desk had an inkstand and a socket for a candle fixed in it.

I was drafted into the youngest class; a place was assigned to me, and a simple lesson given me to learn. Rather subdued by the raw chill of the morning, and the solitariness of being amongst so many busy, indifferent strangers, I was glad enough to hide in my box, and watch the curious effect of all those dim flaring candles in the dawn, and the odd shadows flittering on the whitewashed walls. At half-past seven the doors were opened, and the English girls being collected in one room, prayers were hurriedly read by the English teacher; the same ceremony was, meantime, gone through by the French. Then we filed across the court, to breakfast in a large bare apartment, called *le réfectoire*. A benedicite was said standing, and then we scrambled into our respective seats, the tables extending twice the length of the room, with benches at either side. On sitting down I observed that all the plates on my side were furnished with three tartines a-piece, while those opposite were empty. Down the centre of the table were placed at intervals, wooden trenchers with high-piled slices of bread and butter. The meaning of those pieces was no mystery to me. I had heard of stinting, but had no intention of submitting to it in my own person; so I stretched out my audacious little paw, and took possession of a tartine from the trencher nearest to me. If I had fired a pistol, I could not have made a greater explosion. All the little girls immediately began to vociferate unintelligibly. Mademoiselle Laure gesticulated, and a person opposite presented my plate with the three tartines close before my eyes, and enforced some rule very emphatically, by rapping my fingers with it. I took a bite out of my piece, and looked round mildly, which increased the clamour tenfold, whereupon Miss Knipe was appealed to. She came down upon me with great severity of countenance, and explained that girls under fifteen being limited to three tartines, I must submit to the rule also.

"But uncle Sampson said I was to have as much to eat as I wanted," said I, with a coolness worthy of a better occasion.

The name of uncle Sampson, dear harmless old man, acted like a spell. I looked so resolute and quiet, that everybody fancied some special exemption, in the shape of double pay, lurked behind, and I was permitted to help myself. The circumstance being reported to madame, she talked to me about it in private; but I wisely held on to uncle Sampson, and prevailed, which caused madame to say I was a child of a republican spirit. I am proud to say that this prompt rebellion of mine led to the abrogation of the law of stinting.

Breakfast over, we were all rung into school again, where we stayed until twelve, when, during an hour's recreation, the girls went where they would—chiefly into the court, where there was a pale wintry sunshine. I preferred the classe, where I could think how much nicer it was being at home with uncle Sampson and aunt Martha, than here, where nobody cared for me. Presently in came a child crying, with a book and slate.

She sat down on the floor, and began to write with laborious haste, sobbing all the time. She was a pretty fair-haired girl, younger than myself, and somehow I thought I would help her if I could. My offer was accepted eagerly. She had a page *de l'Histoire Ancienne* to copy out twice, a task which I accomplished speedily. She was English.

"How fast you write! I shall often get you to do my lines for me," said the little damsel cheerfully.

I answered nothing; so she took from her pocket two apples, and, after a critical examination of their merits, offered me the smaller one.

"No, thank you; I don't want your apples. Keep them for yourself," said I, putting her hand aside.

She promptly restored the fruit to her pocket, and scudded off to show her task. I heard her afterwards telling some of the other girls how I had helped her. She laughed at me, and expressed it as her opinion that I was rather silly. If I had demanded the larger apple for my services, she would have respected me. The wisdom of this world comes to us by instalments; it would be a deadly moral poison if imbibed in large quantities.

I arrived at school on Thursday. The next day was Friday—meagre day. The meagre days were very frequent at Madame Freschon's. At dinner I was, like the rest, helped to sorrel-soup, which appeared to me to be an infusion of chopped grass in hot water, flavoured and enriched with a suspicion of vinegar. It was detestable. Madame, observing that I did not touch it after the first spoonful, hoped I should like it by-and-by, as it was an *acquired* taste—not, however, to be *acquired* in a day, or until the youthful appetite has a very sharp edge to it. Then followed dishes of haricot-beans, with hard-boiled eggs sliced and strewn sparsely over them. Vinegar also predominated here, and I suspected oil, but I did not try; for I was sure they would be as unpalatable as the soup. I dined, therefore, upon bread, which I steeped in water, and sprinkled with pepper and salt. I fancied it had quite a perfume of sausages. This was my Lenten

fare as long as I stayed at Madame Freschon's.
On other days we had soup, and the meat from
which it was made; sometimes potatoes; and
always bread, in unlimited quantities. On Sundays, a small glass of *vin ordinaire* and a finger-
biscuit closed the mid-day repast. Once, I remember, Madame proposed to give a Yorkshire
dish, in compliment to me, a native of that county.
We looked forward to it anxiously. The festivity
came off on my birthday. The dish was this:
a huge lump of fat bacon boiled in a copper with
cabbages, and all served up in one nauseous mess
upon a gigantic dish. The French girls despised
me for belonging to barbarians, who called that
food; and I got quite into a rage at their taunts.
Madame's treat was a grand failure, which was
always remembered against me as a personal injury.

There was a collation at five o'clock, when each
girl received two tartines. The supper was at
eight, and consisted of the same as breakfast,
namely, milk and water, facetiously styled *bleu
céleste*, and bread and butter. The interval between collation and supper was, in winter, spent in
the *réfectoire*, where we sewed, played loto, or read.

Before we left the table, when the supper was concluded, Madame Duvivier, the head teacher, rose in her place, and asked, in an audible tone,—

" *Qui a le signom négligent?* "

" *Moi, Madame,*" made answer the unlucky wearer of the untidy badge.

" *Qui a le signom Anglais?* "

" *Moi, Madame,*" responded some English girl, convicted of employing her mother-tongue instead of that she came to learn.

" *Qui a le signom mauvais Français?* "

" *Moi, Madame,*" replied a French girl, found guilty of some grammatical lapse.

Each of these delinquents had to commit to memory thirty lines of French prose. These demands were made thrice daily; so that if the unfortunate possessors of the marks did not contrive to pass them, their lines accumulated fast before the end of the week, as I know to my cost; for I nearly always had one or more. On Saturday, all arrears had to be made up, that day being one of recreation or work, according as we were idle girls, or the reverse.

Penalties were numerous: for being down late ;

for upsetting ink; for tearing any book; for
speaking English; for speaking bad French; and,
at certain seasons, for speaking at all.   Each
had its due punishment.   But the iniquity of ini-
quities was escalading the green gate, which was
locked when we left our bedrooms in the morning, and forbidden to be passed without a special
permit from Madame, until we returned to them
at night.   I was troubled with a fastidious liking
for ablutions before dinner, and, for a long while,
escaladed the gate daily with impunity; but at
last I was caught; and Madame locked me up
for two hours in the drawing-room, where I
looked at her album, and read a volume of an
English novel.   Madame talked to me seriously
before releasing me from this agreeable dur-
ance; but as she laid it on my honour never to
transgress again, I ever afterwards washed my
hands at the little conduit in the court, which
was clear as crystal and cold as ice, and
dried them in the Turkish fashion, by waving in
the air.

Our masters were four: Monsieur Dubufe for
music; Monsieur Pinceau for drawing; Signor

Mori for Italian; and Monsieur Entrechat for dancing. My first introduction to them covered me with ignominy, and was ever afterwards the cause of irritating allusion from Monsieur Dubufe, who was a black, saturnine man, smelling always of garlic and tobacco, and whom I hated.

It was on this wise. Saturday morning was the time for mending rent garments; and, as my ill-luck would have it, I tore a great hole in my stocking with escalading the green gate on Friday morn. It was discovered, and Mademoiselle Laure ordered me to repair it. I sat down to my task in dismay, wishing for dear aunt Martha to help me; but, as wishing would not bring her, I followed the suggestions of my common sense, and set a patch diagonally across the hole. When Mademoiselle Laure saw what I had done, instead of commending me, she burst forth into a tirade, and called me *tout-à-fait sauvage*, then ordered me to carry my handiwork to Madame in her salon below. I was obliged to obey, and went reluctantly enough, for one of my compatriots whispered that I should catch it.

"*Entrez!*" cried Madame when I feebly knocked, and I entered. The four masters were there—being paid, I suppose; and as I had never seen them before, I retreated, saying in English that I would come again. But escape was not so easy. Madame impatiently bade me advance, and taking the stocking from my helpless hand, looked at it with unfeigned horror. I felt all over red-hot, and wished the brick floor would open and engulf me—but it did not. I bit my nether lip, but would not cry—not even when Madame handed the stocking to Monsieur Dubufe, who laughed over it—the monster! The Signor, who was a gentleman, said something kind to me; but I did not understand his words, and little Entrechat shook his head and smiled. I tried to take the stocking from Madame; but, when I had got it, she ordered me to undo my work, and kept me at her elbow while I did it over again. A nice bit of cobbling it was when done; and, as I at last got away, I heard that odious Monsieur Dubufe laugh like a vampire or a ghoul.

Madame Freschon's birthday was always signa-

lized by the presentation of a gift, to which each
girl contributed, according to her liberality or
her means. This ceremony was followed either
by a dance or a theatrical representation. During
the time I was there it was the latter. A sacred
drama was selected. I forget its name; but if
I recollect aright, it was a composition of Madame
Duvivier's, with music by Mons. Dubufe. Of
its literary merits I can say nothing; I only remember that Mademoiselle Laure went mad in
it, and that in the distribution of the *rôles* the
character of David, a shepherd-boy, was portioned
out to me. I took it gleefully; for I thought
it would be great fun. I had one long speech
to learn, and the rest of my part consisted in
holding a small gilt lyre (lent by Mons. Pinceau), and sitting on a bank of green baize,
musing amongst imaginary flocks, beneath a
glowing sky of blue glazed muslin. There was
much excitement and much talk about dresses
and the company; and some criticisms of each
other, not altogether free from sarcasm.

In a month, everybody's part was perfect;
and on Saturday, the grand rehearsal was to

come off in the grenier, all of us being attired
in the dresses in which we were to act. I had
not seen mine during the progress of making,
for everything had to be kept out of Madame's
sight; and when I was taken into Madame Duvivier's chamber, to be invested with it, previous
to appearing on the imaginary stage in the gre--
nier, such a storm of rebellion rose in my heart
at the sight of it, as threatened a blank for the
character of David. It was a kilt—tunic, they
called it—made of Turkey-red calico, profusely
spangled with gilt paper, stuck on with gum.
A broad gauze sash, white and gilt, was to be
tied round my waist. My hair was to be curled
on my neck, and confined by a fillet of gold
paper; a crook in my hand; long silk stockings
and no shoes completed the attire. I looked
at it, and said that no power on earth should
make me put on that thing, meaning the kilt;
but Madame Duvivier flew into a passion, and
screamed that she would not have everything
spoiled by a little " wild English," like me; and
finding ready assistance in her aiders and abettors
in the making of the kilt, I was speedily divested

of my natural garments, and in spite of resistance, manual, pedal, and lingual, attired in the
detested properties of David, a shepherd-boy.
They tried to touch my vanity by telling me
that I made a sweet boy. Madame Duvivier
(she had a moustache, and looked like a dragoon)
kissed me impetuously; and then, as a final appeal,
carried me—secretly covered up with a cloak
—into Madame Freschon's room, that I might
behold myself in her great mirror. The effect
was not what they anticipated. Directly I saw
myself I went down on my knees, and began
to weep and cry out that I would not be dressed
like that—I would have a frock on! They tried
to make me hear reason, by asking, if I had
ever heard of a shepherd-boy tending his flocks
in white muslin? which I answered by asking,
if they had ever heard of one in Turkey-red
calico, with gilt spangles? Madame Duvivier
said I was a savage; and, after a little consultation, I was dragged up to the grenier, where
Mademoiselle Laure, with her long black hair
down to her knees, was raving.

My part came in there: I had to calm her

frenzy by playing on the lyre, and reciting my speech with agreeable and soothing gestures. I was pushed towards her by Madame, who, in an awful voice, ordered me to commence. Lyre in hand I stood, and, in a faint voice, began my charming; but I charmed the reverse of wisely. I had got to the end of the second line, when Miss Knipe screamed out, " Little David, stand on both legs! " A titter ensued. I had got my left foot curled up round my right knee. I went on, growing more nervous every moment; until, about midway, Madame Duvivier yelled ferociously, " David, if you does not put down dat ittle leg, I tie it to de ground! "

The titter became a laugh—the tragedy a comedy; the mad woman was convulsed, and the audience too. They saw it would not do. So I was stripped of my finery, and a French girl of my size being invested with it, went through the *rôle* with great boldness and success.

On another great holiday, Madame Freschon thought that, instead of the usual games in the court, we had better take a walk into the country. Nothing loth, we set out, two by two, each with

her chosen companion. Mine was a French girl,
Laurence by name, a queer creature, with a long
moveable nose and wild spirits. As we walked,
I gave her an account of the meeting of Henry
the Eighth and Francis the First on the Field
of the Cloth of Gold, embellishing it with little
incidents not mentioned in history, but perhaps
none the less true for that. We were then trudg-
ing along the road which runs through this
memorable field; and suddenly the idea struck
us that it would be pleasant to walk as far as
Ardres: no sooner conceived than suggested aloud
to those behind and before. Some said it was
five miles, others that it was eight; one remembered that Madame Freschon's sister had given
us a general invitation to visit her at all oppor-
tunities, and that our presence would therefore
be most welcome. We had six hours before
dark. In short, the fates were propitious, the
teacher undecided, and we imperious—we would
go! The line of march had been broken up
during the debate, and it was not re-formed. Some
of us made little excursions into the fields to
gather wild flowers as mementoes of our walk;

others tramped up and down that tantalizing suc-
cession of little rises and falls in the road, with
a respectable, solid perseverance, which showed
a strong innate sense of duty. Ardres seemed
a terribly long way off; but the rest we anticipated, and the galettes which Madame's sister
would be sure to give us, sustained us when
inclined to weary. At last we saw a wall, a
gateway, houses, a little river, and women wash-
ing clothes in it—Ardres. Through the gateway we went into a queer old street; and in-
quiring our way, found the house we sought
near the market-place. I believe that at this time
(it was the hour for the collation) we had forgotten all historical and romantic histories, and
thought chiefly of galettes. The door was a long
time in being opened, and then the Flemish servant, to our unutterable disgust, said her mistress
was not at home! Some murmured aloud; others
stoically faced about, and marched out of the
town, declaring that nobody should ever catch
them at Ardres again. I felt misanthropic,
hungry, and footsore; Laurence was crossly and
mischievously vivacious. We looked and felt

like a garrison reduced to capitulate on hard
terms. And to add to our distress, now that
our faces were set towards home, there was the
cruel anticipation of what Madame Freschon would
say when we arrived there. The little girls were
very tired, and some even cried. Laurence
carried one on her back for nearly a mile, but
then she could go no farther, and the child
walked the rest of the way, fretting and making
us feel dreadfully remorseful. When we were
within a couple of miles of home, and it was
growing dark, we met Madame's father coming
to meet us. How our hearts sank!—but only
to rise with a delicious rebound when, on entering the gates, we were received with a motherly
blandness, inconceivable to me under the circumstances. The supper was all ready, and we were
pressed to partake of it even by Madame Duvivier,
who was usually so grim. Prayers and bed were
naturally expected to follow: but no, vain hope!
our transgression was not to go unpunished. As
soon as the Benedicite was said, with a sweet,
satisfied smile on her countenance and the most
natural air in the world, Madame rose and cried :

"*En classe, mesdemoiselles.*"

Crushed and dismayed, we all went into our departments, and were compelled to do the afternoon's lessons. That over, the greater number went to bed; but the Italian class, of which I was one, was still detained to prepare our work for the signor on the morrow. The only revenge we had left us was pretending not to be tired, and exchanging lively remarks: but Madame Duvivier would not be aggravated: she saw through the manœuvre.

We never took holiday again.

From the Diary.

THIS morning, Emmy being engaged in a botanical lesson, I invited myself to take a constitutional
walk with Miss Mostyn and Belle. Miss Mostyn
is a sensible, conscientious woman, and I am
glad to find that Belle and she have taken to
each other so thoroughly; for some of my friends,
Mrs. Harding especially, are changing governesses every few months, which must be disad-
vantageous both to teacher and taught. Miss
Mostyn and I have spoken before upon this
vexed question of governesses and their em-
ployers; and this morning, I having introduced
the subject with reference to Mrs. Harding's requiring a lady to instruct her children
after the Christmas vacation, she gave me the
benefit of her own experiences before she came
to Wortlebank.

From first to last she must have had a pretty hard battle of it. She is thirty now; methodical, quiet, and very grey; no one would suspect that she had once been of a lively, animated beauty, which from a miniature of herself that came to her at her mother's death I can perceive she was—or of a cheerful, buoyant temper—it is the sort of life, she says, that destroys that very early. By the by, she is *not* thirty, though she looks it to the full—she told me on her last birthday that she was twenty-six. I cannot quite cordially acquiesce in all she says, but it is too true that the personal comfort of governesses is extremely little thought of; yet single women love things pretty and pleasant about them. Miss Mostyn lays her own indifferent health to the charge of the two years she spent at Fleetham Parsonage, where she lived entirely in her school-room, which looked, not into the open air, but into a stone passage where plants were housed in the winter. This room in damp weather had such an evil odour from bad drainage that the children were never allowed to remain there, except for the few hours of study; but Miss

Mostyn, who was not expected to join the family
circle, had to endure it; and as a precaution
against the disagreeable odour she contrived to
fix her vinaigrette on the tip of her nose, and to
wear it even when writing or sewing. This was
laughed at as a clever device; but no idea was
entertained of giving her a fit apartment until
the medical man, who characterized the room she
had as "one degree livelier than looking down
a well," said that she must either give up her
situation, or it would presently give up her.

The schoolroom Mrs. Harding sets apart—
close under the slates—is a very unsuitable
place for children as well as for their teacher;
no wonder the latter complains almost daily
of headache. In winter the room cannot be
efficiently warmed from the smallness of the
stove, and in summer it is as hot as an oven.
It is a mistake to think that *anything will do*
for the governess; the mind becomes dull and
heavy that has only children's society and displeasing environments. I feel very glad that the
sunny south room over the hall was given for
the schoolroom here as soon as one was called

for; it always looks bright and cheerful when I
go in, and nobody who saw Miss Mostyn's pretty
arrangements of books and flowers could ever
imagine her a person to reconcile herself to an
ugly, comfortless domicile—indeed, she says
candidly that she never remained in any house
where her personal surroundings were treated
as matters of no moment.

Some of her remarks a little amuse me. She
says people have written books about governesses,
and have invested them—or tried to do so—
with an interest that they have not got; and,
generally speaking, they have done them more
harm than good. The only character of the
kind that she acknowledges to be satisfactory is
Miss Cann—a clever, shrewd, sharp-spoken, plain
little woman, with just enough sentiment about
her to be a woman and not a machine.

She says nothing of wounded feelings in connection with her position, and evidently thinks
that view over-worked; but what she does complain of is the wretched pay. Until she came
here her salary was never more than thirty
pounds, out of which she cannot have saved

much. She began to teach at seventeen, and may go on till seventy, after which, she says, she shall retire into a little room, and exist, barely enough, on the scrapings of her salaries and two meals a day, as the superannuated sisterhood is in the habit of ·doing. When one considers this result as the probable one to which so many hard-working lives tend, can we marvel that governesses are so often low-spirited complainers?

Yesterday arrived Steenie from Westminster, buoyant with prizes! He has been working hard, and does not look so strong as he ought, but home and outdoor sports will soon bring back the honest colour to his face. Harry went from Oxford first for a few days' visit to his grandpapa, but he is to be down here on Christmas Eve. Jean and Francis Maynard come over before the new year and bring their Blanche. I have also asked my ancient friend Miss Bootle to forsake the old maids for a week or two, and to travel here and enliven herself

amongst our young folks. All the children are
fond of Miss Bootle. She wears everlastingly,
and was as gay and prancing when I saw her
last summer as I remember her at my first going
to Crofton more than thirty years ago.

Mr. Dover and Emmy are prosecuting their
botanical studies, as usual, this morning. I cannot say that I have been much struck by any
novelty in the specimens Emmy brings in to dry,
but I believe she never gathers any until the
lesson is nearly over, and so it is possible that
she misses many valuable ones which more conscientious research would bring to light. Their
engagement is now no longer a secret, and I think
it has been a surprise to some of our friends.
Mrs. Travis told me candidly that *she* thought
Emmy might have looked higher than her father's
curate, lovely as she is universally acknowledged
to be, and a granddaughter of the bishop besides.

" And what *has* Mr. Dover ? " she asked me.

I said he had to my mind the qualities that
make a wife happy, which appear to me to be in
this case the most important consideration of all.
I know what she meant. Mr. Dover is not a man

of property, but Emmy has a very good fortune from her mother, and it matters little on which side the money is, so long as there is union of character and affection. Felix, I know, has not given it a thought. When Belle was born he told me that he was going to effect a second insurance on his life for her benefit, remarking that Emmy was provided for, and that Belle when she was grown up should not have my old excuse for using any man who loved her as I used him. It is sometimes doubtful to me whether Felix has quite forgiven my foolish perversity. I have heard him inveigh strongly against the wrong of sacrificing happiness to an idea, and *once* on the *fantastical conceit* of self-martyrdom. I can afford not to care now; but I am very glad my dear girls will not have my temptations or trials to battle with; for the years of our lives are too brief and precious to be wasted in futile efforts to do a better duty than God has set plain before our eyes.

What a cloud has all at once fallen on our happy home!

While Hannah and I were this morning discussing the accommodation of our guests, who begin to arrive early next week, Felix came to the dressing-room door, and said he wished to have a little talk with me down in the library. He had a letter in his hand which the post had brought since breakfast, and which I saw at a glance was from Harry.

Felix looked troubled, and I feared that something was seriously amiss. He pushed my chair near the fire, which he had suffered to get very low, and then said, rather abruptly,—

" Well, Kathie, you are pleased with your son-in-law that is to be; but how are you prepared to welcome a *daughter-in-law?*"

" You don't mean to tell me that Harry is *married*, Felix?" cried I, in inexpressible surprise.

"He is married, Kathie; no mistake about it at all," and Felix passed me the letter.

Harry has been married nearly eighteen months, and has a baby boy!

The confession seemed at first so ridiculous that

I could hardly help smiling, but when it recurred
to me how he had come home to Wortlebank,
vacation after vacation, with this secret upon him,
deceiving his father who loved and trusted him
in all things, I felt that he had done a cruel as
well as a foolish act.

Felix was profoundly hurt—so keenly wounded
that even to me he could not bear to talk about it
more. When I had read the letter he bade me
carry it away and tell Emmy. I have not told
her yet; I want to consider the announcement
maturely, and to set it before her in its least
painful light.

Poor Harry was always wilful, passionate and
imperious, but most warm-hearted and affectionate
in disposition. He is as dear to me as my own
Steenie. I see how he has got into his present
position. He must have fallen violently in love,
and, hurried away by his feelings into an ill-con-
sidered marriage, he was afraid to acknowledge
it. He need not to have been afraid, poor boy;
anything is almost more readily forgiven than a
long course of deception. He was, it appears,
barely twenty-one when he took upon himself the

dignities and responsibilities of married life. His letter is not at all humble or conciliatory; it has evidently been "got over" under his young wife's urging as something disagreeable that had to be done, and that was only made more difficult by every day's delay. He has been at the bishop's only two days, and at the time of writing was in lodgings near London with his family!

Harry's family! it is a picture almost too hard for my imagination to depict, and as I think of it, a hundred questions rise in my mind. How has he maintained his young wife, for we have heard of no debts, no extravagance? Who is she? Who are her kinsfolk? Is she the girl Harry should have given to Emmy for a sister?

But what avail conjectures? We shall know all by and by.

I told Hannah last night of poor Harry's grievous sins of omission and commission; and to my indignation, the idea of his little son has taken such a powerful hold on her mind, that to every

reprehensive remark I advance she only replies,—

"Why not? Let 'em marry! it's what they
came into the world for! To think that I should
live to see my dear missis's great-grandson!
And what's his christened name, may I ask,
ma'am?"

"His christened name is not known at Wortlebank; to us he is 'Harry's baby,' and nothing
more."

I gave Emmy his letter to read, and she ob-
stinately refuses to acknowledge that he has done
any wrong: her admiration and reverence for
Harry are intense, and *she* is angry that anybody should be angry with *him*. Her first act
was to write off a long letter, full of love and
sympathy, which she showed to me before post-
ing it. I saw no objection, so it was sent: I
daresay he will feel it more than the hardest
reproaches. But Felix cannot pass over his conduct so lightly,—he never showed anything but
the tenderest love and consideration for all his
children, and Harry's ingratitude is a sharp
pang. Had there been coldness or severity

in his treatment of him there might be some
excuse; but now there is none. He has not
written to the poor lad yet, and I can see the
once-pleasure has become a most painful and
irksome task.

I have the greatest dread of family disunion, and
that must not come amongst us if it can by any
means be avoided. Hannah was saying to me
this morning that she supposed now Mr. Harry
must leave his little old room and be promoted
to a larger,—where was she to put him? and
had she not better have the cot brought down
from the green garret, and put in proper order
before his arrival with his *family?* when Felix
came in, and hearing the drift of the question,
said coldly,—

" Your young master will not spend his Christmas at Wortlebank this year, Hannah."

I looked up at him with pleading tears, and
" Oh, Felix!" but he would not listen even
to me.

Since the children have been given to understand that Harry is not to come home, they have
all shown themselves indignant.

"What has he done? is there anything wrong
in getting married?" says Steenie.

"It will be no Christmas at all without Harry!"
cries Belle; and Emmy, who feels where he has
erred against his father, does nothing but fret.
Felix says no more.

The fiat has gone forth. Harry is not to spend
his Christmas at Wortlebank this year.

I have no hope of changing his resolution,
because he thinks it right to show his displeasure
in this way. Hannah dared to tell him that *his*
mother would not have dealt so by *him*; and my
philosophy is, that when a deed is done and un-
alterable, it is both Christian and expedient to
begin at once to make the best instead of the
worst of it.

Felix wrote to Harry this morning, and gave
me the letter to read before he sent it. It was
very kind even in its severity, and I know how

it will work on the lad's heart and conscience; and how he will feel his almost just exclusion from amongst us for a season. When darling Emmy learnt that there was to be no relenting, she shed a bitter flood of tears, and declared it was cruel.

She has been telling Mr. Dover all about it since luncheon, and he has asked for three days, including Sunday, to take a run up to town. I conjecture that he is going for the sole purpose of seeing Harry, and bringing her tidings; but as she does not mention it, I do not feel it necessary to intrude into their confidence; or it may be that Mr. Dover has undertaken the journey from his own interest and kindness to Harry; for they were always dear friends from the curate's first coming to Wortlebank; I almost wonder Harry did not confide his difficulties to him earlier, and make use of him as a mediator with his father.

This event has quite spoilt our looking forward to Christmas, which began so happily with dear Emmy's engagement. The house is very quiet, as if a misfortune had happened in it, or deadly

sickness were tenanting one of its chambers.
Only Hannah's voice is raised in ire more frequently and sharply than I ever heard it before.
She feels personally injured by Harry's banishment; and though she does not fail in outward
respect to her master, she accords it with an air
of the most reproachful dignity, and bestows
obtrusive, pathetic assiduities on Emmy, whom
she considers almost, but not quite, as much
wronged as herself.

Hannah has taken herself off to London! She
presented herself in my room this morning
cloaked and bonneted, and with a carpet-bag in
her hand, before I was dressed. She announced
formally that she was going—she could not bear
to see things "all askew," and so she should be
better out of the way, where she could not be
vexed. And if those whose duty it was to look
after Master Harry meant to neglect him—well,
he should know there was *one body*, at least,
that would not forget what was owing to him.

The real secret of her sudden start is anxiety for the baby. I daresay it has suffered a hundred deaths through carelessness and ignorance, in her imagination, since she heard of its existence; she believes nobody understands the management of children but herself, and has a pride in ·being nurse-tender to a third generation. When I saw she was utterly bent on going, I gave up opposing her, and said that when she found herself ceasing to be useful to Harry, we should be glad to welcome her back.

"I'll come back when Master Harry comes, and not one minute afore," was her sturdy but sorrowful reply. " And will you tell the master that I never expected it to come to this—that he would shut the door in his son's face—at Christmas time, of all the year! I've no heart to speak to him again myself, for I can well see that his back's up."

Felix says I ought not to have suffered her to go; but how was I to prevent it? Hannah is growing aged, but she does not seem to have abated one iota of her natural force and will. She has always been my right hand in the house, and my authority has never been exercised either over or against her; she is a person to have her own way. But for the cold weather coming on so suddenly, I should have secretly rejoiced that she was gone to Harry, for I have my fears about how the little one will fare between those two young things, its father and mother. However, Hannah is hardy, and I shall hope for the best until I hear news to the contrary.

Miss Bootle comes to-morrow; I shall be glad to see my old friend; for with this trouble and aggravation of feeling amongst us, the presence of a comparative stranger in the house will make the season slip over with less marked difference to ordinary Christmases.

We have not seen any of our neighbours since the news spread, but I can imagine their censures.

This day has been wearily long; we have not the heart to talk, or anticipate pleasant things; and it was almost a relief when Belle summoned us to the schoolroom at four o'clock for another reading from the Portfolio.

The story she had chosen was "The Heir of Hardington." Miss Bootle arrived just as it was finished.

THE HEIR OF HARDINGTON.

I.

When Sir Willoughby Monke of Hardington and Frogholmes died, he left two daughters—co-heiresses. The estates, each lying in a different county, were not to be dismembered for equal division, but to be drawn by lot according to his will.

Cecily, the elder daughter, got Hardington in Yorkshire; Frogholmes, left to Eliza, the younger, was in the Fens of Lincolnshire. Within eighteen months of their father's death both the heiresses married, bestowing name and fortune on their respective husbands, for the name of Monke was to go always with the property, which was strictly entailed on any children that the sisters might bear. The marriages were equally discreet and

common-place.   Mr. Percival and Mr. Cholmondeley became Monkes without hesitation, and
entered on the regency of their wives' estates with
sedate satisfaction and the general good opinion
of their neighbours.   Their known wealth notwithstanding, the sisters had never been popular
or much sought after.

They were plain young women ; short and in-
elegant in figure, and with ordinary blunt features,
small eyes, scanty light hair, and indifferent com-
plexions.   They had received narrow educations
even for that time, and håd no natural enlarge-
ment of mind to make up for defects of training.
They had, however, a few decided opinions,
amongst which were these : Hardington and Frogholmes were the finest estates in the kingdom ;
Monke was the most distinguished name in the
red books; Cecily and Eliza Monke were the
most to be envied of all the heiresses in the whole
wide world.   With such sublime and happy
views of themselves and their belongings, the
sisters could not fail to be reasonably amiable ;
apart from a stolid obstinacy in the elder, and a
craving selfishness in the younger, they were

amiable. They were very peaceable wives in a
house, but then they ruled, and their husbands
obeyed. This was the conjugal arrangement
from the beginning—the wisest arrangement
under the circumstances.

When Cecily married Mr. Percival she was
seven and twenty; a woman without romance,
without tenderness, without geniality, sympathy,
or any of the little loveable traits which are the
vital breath of domestic life. A man might
almost as well take a stone into his bosom as such
a piece of animated clay for a wife. Mr. Percival
Monke was not a great character, but he had
enough of the leaven of humanity in him to
experience very considerable annoyance from
Cecily's coldness. He had been rather taken by
her orderliness and system, by her care of her
father, and her pride of station, and, though not
in love, he thought she would make him a
suitable partner. He was disappointed; but a
few failures convinced him of the fruitlessness of
attempting to work any change in her, so he be-
took himself to field pursuits, and went often from
home, while she droned on her placid, self-con-

centrated way, buried alive at Hardington, neither receiving nor paying visits when they could be avoided.

Mr. and Mrs. Cholmondeley Monke's life was not unlike that led by Cecily and her husband at first; but afterwards, perhaps under pressure of boredom, perhaps from more vivacity of temper and less principle, Mr. Cholmondeley broke out into certain excesses which speedily cramped the revenues of Frogholmes. Cecily, indignant that Eliza had not governed her spouse better, declined to receive either of them at Hardington, and was as glad as her temperament permitted her to be when they forsook the Fens and went to live abroad.

For several years neither sister bore children, but, at last, Eliza wrote to announce a daughter, and in reply Cecily sent word that three months before she had blessed Hardington with a son and heir.

II.

THE Heir of Hardington. Lord of the Manor of Hardington. Francis George Percival Monke, Lord of the Manor of Hardington.

Such was his mother's view of the wizened, monkey-faced boy she had brought into the world. Never "my baby," "my poor little weakling baby," never "joy," or "love," or "pet," or "pride," or "delight," but always Heir of Hardington, Lord of the Manor of Hardington,—representative of so many acres and so much money, and so many neglected responsibilities.

Poor little Francis George Percival Monke! How he was doctored and iron-framed, and mother-tutored, and private tutored, and padded, and bolstered, and be-praised! No baby of any sagacity but would have made haste to die under such an ordeal, even had it been preparatory to the inheritance of the united kingdoms of Great Britain and Ireland. But Francis George, being a dull boy, lived through it, and, at twelve years old, was about as foolish, as conceited, and as helpless a lad as the race of Monke ever produced. By that time he had outgrown the iron frame, and could walk straight on his feeble limbs; he could also repeat every particular of the estate he was to inherit; tell you its value under the old leases, and what it might be made to produce when the said leases fell in; and also he could exact reverence to himself from tenant and servant as their master in embryo. His father said he was a fool.

There was a grain of good in him, of course, as there is in every heart, God-planted, until the devil-sown tares of the world spring up to choke it. He would not inflict pain, and was sorry to see pain; he was kind to animals; he was not ungenerous, and he worshipped his mother. She never caressed him—never indulged him. " You ought to do this," "you must learn to do that," " such and such honour is your due and your right;" were speeches constantly on her lips, though never accompanied with an incitement to any high or noble rule of life. If she had lost him, she would have grieved for him as the lost heir of Hardington—not as her one child whose birth-pangs had almost cost her life.

She taught him her notion of the duties of property practically; and, as her notion was how to get most money out of it, and how to put the least into it, his views did not become very liberal or extended. For him there was a sermon in each stone of the village of Hardington—a village not pretty by any means, nor well-ordered, nor well-moralled, nor well-mannered, but still quite good enough for Mrs. Percival Monke, so long as the cottagers were punctual with their rent.

When honest folk rhapsodize of rural innocence and peace and comfort, they don't picture to themselves villages of the Hardington type. They dream of bowery dwellings redolent of sweet flowers; of bees and honey, and clotted cream, and dainty rashers, and fresh eggs, and delicious cakes. They dream of rosy-cheeked Phyllis with her milking-pail at the stile, and some handsome swain courting her. They dream of a poet's Utopia, or a new broom-swept hamlet, or a depen-dency of a rich and generous feudal lord; but there are many Hardingtons in the world that cannot be made to answer to their happy delusion at all;—Hardingtons, where fathers and mothers bring up indiscriminate tribes of children in two-roomed tumble-down dwellings; where they get coarse bread, and not enough of that, the week in and the week out; where, if innocence remains, she remains in spite of evil and temptation; where vice breeds crime in a hotbed of ignorance; where rheumatism and fever are everyday guests, and the squire and the people are each other's natural enemy.

This was much the case on the fine estate to which Francis George Percival Monke had the misfortune to be born heir, and his mother's precepts were not likely to help him to improve it. A narrow-minded, bigoted, purse-proud woman, be she mother or be she wife, is one of the greatest hindrances that can befall a man; and, in his youth, Francis George certainly showed none of that force of character which might have promised that he would, some day, strike out an independent and better line of conduct for himself.

III.

There is no knowing into what depths of stulti-
fied folly the lad might have meandered, but for
a lucky accident that befell him when he was
about sixteen. He was riding an ill-broken pony
through the village of Grenside, when it took
fright and ran away with him, threw him, and
broke his arm. The youth was picked up and
carried into the house of the curate of the parish,
whose wife put him to bed and sent for his mother
and the doctor. The doctor came and set the
limb, and his mother came to nurse him,—but
finding her own comforts restricted in the curate's
abode, she soon left him to recover without her
attendance. She acted advisedly; Francis George
could not have been in better hands.

Mr. Proby was a plain, steady-going, worthy
clergyman, and his wife was an excellent woman;
a woman of talent and education, of enthusiasm
and genuine warm-heartedness. Curate-like, Mr.
Proby had a house full of children; hearty,
noisy, generous, mischievous boys, and laughter-

loving, pretty girls. All the family were good-looking, but Katie was a real beauty, a copy of her mother; nearly, if not quite, as handsome as her mother had been at the same age. There was no nonsense about Katie; no silly affectation of boyishness, no still sillier affectation of premature womanishness. She was a thorough girl, tall, slight, agile—as swift a runner, and as good a climber, skipper, and general playfellow as brothers could wish for; and yet she was an adept at her needle, a good nurse, a clever little scholar, and a most sunshiny companion to everybody. A great part of the attendance upon Francis George fell to her share, and she did it with a cheerful alacrity and kindness all her own.

There was not much about the young gentleman to attract liking; he did not become a favourite in the family by any means; the smaller Proby children disliked him, in fact; and even their mother, kind as she was, found him too exacting and imperious an inmate to be civil to longer than necessary : so, as soon as he was sufficiently recovered to return home, he was not pressed to stay longer. Every one took leave of him rather gladly than otherwise—Katie included.

Going back to Hardington was a return to polar regions. Francis George missed something. He missed the atmosphere of warm affection that surrounded the curate's hearth, and made his family as one; he missed the cheerful voices and laughter, and, above all, he missed Katie's smile and good-humoured attentions. His mother was like a machine, after those impulsive Probys. Francis George tried to thaw her by telling her stories of the ways and customs of the curate's house, but he might as easily have hoped to thaw the old stone griffins at Hardington gate by breathing on them, as to thaw her by any such process. She became by and by quite impatient of any allusion to his friends, and told him that his gratitude was absurdly overstretched.

Yes; Francis George had a fund of obstinate, pertinacious, unforgetting gratitude in his disposition, which this lucky accident developed. It was the nearest approach to any decided virtue that he had yet displayed. His father and mother had insisted on compensating Mrs. Proby

for the trouble and expense of their son's re-
covery, but Francis George could not be per-
suaded to look upon it as a cancelling of his debt.
He turned his pony's head towards Grenside
nearly every day, and inquired after the health
of the Probys, as if, instead of being a hardy
race, they were a family of chronic invalids.
Katie used to go out to the gate laughing, to
answer his questions and receive his messages;
and one day, with a fiery blush on his face and
a nervous stammer in his voice, he told her he
had brought her a little present.

"You must not let my mother know, but I
spent all my quarter over it," said he, in a
hurried whisper, trying to put a morocco case
into her hands; but Katie, clasping those little
members behind her back, shook her head in a
resolute way, and said she must not accept pre-
sents from him; papa would not like it; especially
if Mrs. Percival Monke did not know.

"Oh! but do, Katie! I should never have
bought it but for you—it is a watch and chain!"
persisted he, with anxious earnestness. In the
first place, it had cost him an immense effort of

self-denial to make the purchase at all; and in
the second, he had been full a month in raising
up his courage to offer it—it was cruel indeed to
reject it, and his " do, Katie! " was most pathetic.

" No, no, no! " she replied; " you ought not
to have spent your money in such a foolish
way."

" It is not foolish. Look here, Katie! I like
you better than anybody in the world, except my
mother : that I do ! You're so good ! "

Katie ran away laughing, with her hands over
her ears : the more he called to her to stop, the
more she would not.

" Katie, if you won't have it, I'll throw it
into the mill-dyke! " he cried, at last; and as
she still paid no heed, he turned round towards
home, and was as good or as bad as his word.

For more than a week after this rebuff he
did not appear at Grenside at all. He was apparently offended by Katie's very proper refusal
of his gift. She had told her mother the whole
story—the threat about the mill-dyke included;
but neither believed he would be so wild as to
put it into execution; so that, when one of the

Proby boys came home exultant, with the morocco case in his hand, proclaiming that he had found it amongst the long reeds on the bank, they were unfeignedly surprised. They had not given Francis George credit for so much spirit, and both of them liked him the better for this foolish extravagant flight. Katie, by her father's orders, even wrote him a kind little letter, when the watch was sent back to him.

The next day he came to see them again, making no allusion either to the watch or to his long absence, and then regularly resumed his calls with active constancy. The Probys, one and all, were very kind to him,—but oh! what foolish speeches he used to make about his property, his dignity, and himself! How he did bore poor Katie and her mother over their work-table, when he tangled every reel, and disordered every box and basket that came within his reach. He had a stupid tutor at home, who taught him a little Latin and Greek; but left him as ignorant of commonplace, useful knowledge as a Fejee islander. If you had asked him where America was, or whether it was land or water or cream-cheese, he could not have told you.

He had a complacent, good-humoured self-conceit, that cushioned him softly against contempt and pity. Glorified as he was at home, how could he suspect that he was laughed at abroad? —that even Katie Proby laughed at him, though she pitied him, and rather liked his stupid kindliness of temper?

It was an awful shock to the heir of Hardington when, a long time after, he offered his hand, his heart, and his futurity to the poor curate's daughter, and was refused. He was in real, hard earnest, poor long-limbed, feeble-minded fellow; and when Katie blushed rather angrily, and said " No," in a curt, unmistakable tone, the tears fairly came into his eyes.

" I thought you liked me, Katie,—haven't I been coming here for years? You don't know, I can't tell you how fond I am of you! I'd do anything for you, Katie, that I would ! My mother knows I would," spluttered he, with frightful energy.

" I'm so sorry, Francis George, I am so very

sorry," replied Katie, a little frightened and subdued.

"It is of no use to be sorry; if you don't
like me, you can't help it, and I don't care what
becomes of me if you don't. But it is too bad.
I could not have believed it!"

This anti-climax to his emotion almost made
Katie smile; but, checking the impulse, she pretended to hear her mother calling to her, and
left her discomfited suitor alone.

Francis George Percival Monke was only nine-
teen when he thus exhibited himself, and had
never left his mother's apron-strings for a single
day.

IV.

Mr. and Mrs. Cholmondeley Monke continued
to reside abroad, in more or less discomfort, until
their daughter was of an age to be introduced
into society, and then they brought her home
to England, and, at her aunt's invitation, to
Hardington. The two sisters had made a compact for the reunion of their family property by
marrying their children; and each was formally

told of this compact before they met. Francis George received the announcement in solemn silence, and Flora received it with an expressive giggle and a hope that her cousin was handsome and lively, and not mopish, like so many of the English gentlemen she had seen abroad.

Flora Monke had no hereditary right to be pretty, but she was pretty—even beautiful; and her foreign manners and graces had the air of making her still prettier than she was. Her aunt received her with surly approbation, and Francis George with a stolid composure, which did not promise any keen susceptibility to her charms. She was piqued, and told her mother he was an idiot.

If Flora expected to be courted, and flattered, and worshipped by her cousin, she must have been disappointed, for he kept as much out of her way as ever he could, and never said a civil thing to her; a peculiarity for which his mother took him to task one morning when they were alone. She still treated her son as authoritatively as when he was a boy in tunics.

" Francis George, you are a dull wooer," she

said, with slow sarcasm; "Flora cannot be very proud of you."

"I don't like Flora," replied Francis George, gravely.

"But you must learn to like her, since she is to be your wife——"

"Mother, if Flora Monke was the only woman left in the world, I would not marry her. I don't like her."

Mrs. Percival Monke grew red all over her dull grey face. This was the first word of rebellion and contradiction she had ever heard from her son since he was born; and, if he had struck her, she could not have looked more indignant or surprised.

"Francis George Percival Monke!" she cried, with strangled, choking dignity, "do you know who I am and who you are?"

The young man quaked visibly at her awful voice, but the stolid resolution of his visage did not relax a muscle. He was to the full as obstinate as his mother, and when they clashed on a subject, when each was equally determined, then began the tug of war.

"Yes, mother; I am heir of Hardington, lord
of the manor of Hardington," said he, in that
formula which had been dinned into his ears so
long. It made his mother laugh; for, at this
moment, it sounded ridiculous enough.

"Deplume you of those distinctions, sir, and
do you know what you are then?" said she,
bitterly.

"My father says I am a fool," replied Francis
George; "other people are of a like opinion——"

"Not such a fool as they take you to be," said
his mother. "You have as much sense as nine
men in ten if you will use it, and you must
use it now in overcoming your absurd aversion
to your cousin Flora. I say you shall marry her
—and soon, too!"

"And I say I will not! I am almost of age,
and I shall be my own master in that matter,
at least."

The young man spoke quietly but firmly. His
mother, looking up at his face, felt the reins of
authority slipping from her grasp. Her weak,
awkward, foolish boy was, as it were, become
a man by magic. There he stood before her,

six feet two; lean but sinewy, a face far from
vacuous; expressive, indeed, of a brute courage
and obstinacy, which, being provoked, would
never slumber again. But for his foolish training, he would have been a fine young man;
as it was, he had not active mind enough to
inform that mass of matter. The old habit
of love and fear of his mother was strong
upon him yet; she saw it, and hoped to triumph
still.

"You ought to be glad that Flora will have
you," she said, "and you ought to have a pleasure in re-uniting our dissevered property. If
you do not marry Flora, you may be your own
master, but you shall not be master of anything
else while I live, and when I die you shall have
nothing but the bare estate; that I promise
you."

"I don't care for Hardington. I don't see
any good it has ever done either you or my
father or me. I think it is a miserable place,"
replied Francis George, in perfect good faith.

His mother's eyes fixed on him as if she thought
him a maniac in a dangerous mood.

"Will you be pleased to explain yourself; if you are not raving; which I sadly suspect," said she, fiercely.

"Why, mother, what good has it done us, or anybody?" persisted the heir. "My father is always away in London, and hates it. You sit at work all day as hard as if you worked for bread, and nobody comes near you; and because of it, you would make me marry a girl I don't love. Then there's the village. Such dirty old houses and people, and no schools. If we were paupers instead of people of ten thousand a-year, we could not have a greater heap of misery outside the gates than we have. What is the good of the Hardington money if we don't spend it? I say again, I don't care for Hardington. Mr. Proby's sons are better off than I am; because they have been well brought up and they have got professions. When I am amongst fellows of my age, I feel like a fool, and I am a fool."

"That is a fact beyond doubt," replied his mother, drily. "But don't waste any more breath over decrying Hardington—you shall leave it—

you shall have a profession. Yes! yes! you shall
be an idle gentleman no longer!"

There was a disagreeable tone in this threat,
which made Francis George turn hot and cold
all over. It was a rather critical act of his, this
sudden snapping of the leading-strings in which
he had walked so long and humbly. He felt
vexed, too, in a stupid sort of way, at having
vexed his mother, and was just on the point of
making some concession, when Flora came into
the room—Flora in a gay muslin dress and most
coquettish hat; a maiden to attract a man's fancy,
most people would have thought, but, as it seemed,
not the star that could attract his.

"Flora, our young gentleman takes umbrage
at the gifts of fortune, and despises them—heroic,
is he not?" said Mrs. Percival Monke.

Flora glanced from one to the other with a
puzzled air, and asked what was the matter.
Francis George went out and left his mother to
explain as little or as much as she thought desirable. The consequence of her explanation was,
that the Hardington Monkes and the Frogholmes
Monkes separated coldly the next day, and Flora

went to prosecute her first campaign in town.. Francis George did not care where she went, so long as he was no more troubled with her airs and graces.

V.

THE lawyer who managed the business affairs of the Monkes, was Mr. Leatherhead ; a dry, clever, craft-ingrained old fellow, who greatly admired the elder of the co-heiresses' style of saving and managing her property. He said she had a brain as acute and as hard as most men, and it was a pity her son was so little like her. He thought he knew her pretty well, but even he, for a man of varied experience, was extremely astonished when he received from her the following letter :—

" SIR,—   "Hardington, June 7, 182-.

"I am sure you will lend me your valuable assistance in a project for my son, which I have much at heart. He is bitten by some of those radical views for the regeneration of the poor, which are subverting society in every quarter, and I think a year's confinement in your office may tend more towards his cure than all the reasoning in the world. Make him work as your lowest clerk, and show him no respect or distinction, as that would defeat my views. He shall have no further allowance from me than a clerk's salary at a low rate, and I intend that he should live upon it. The harder he fares, the more likely is he to become sensible of his folly in adopting the philanthropic crotchets of the age. Until he gives them up, I quite renounce him. He will be in town, and at your office, on Thursday next.

"Yours, &c.,

" CECILY P. MONKE."

" Ah ! ah ! " commented the shrewd old lawyer ; " Miss Cecily's plan for uniting Hardington and Frogholmes has gone off—that's the true interpretation of this document. What tyrants women are ! Well ! I suppose I must try to humour both."

Thus it was that Francis George Percival Monke, heir of Hardington, lord of the manor of Hardington, became a lawyer's clerk. His

mother thought he would soon sicken of London
lodgings and Mr. Leatherhead's sedentary work.;
but, contrary to her expectations, and even to her
hopes, he accommodated himself to his new position with cheerfulness and alacrity. He made a
friend amongst his fellow clerks in the person of
young Willie Proby, and the pair took rooms in
the same house, and lived together like brothers.

"Francis George is no fool!" said old Leatherhead to himself. "He is a better fellow and
a more sensible fellow than any of us thought.
It is that silly mother of his who has had her
own ends to serve by keeping him in the background."

Yes. Francis George began to develop a plain,
useful kind of ability; he had no genius, but he
had concentrativeness, and a very straightforward
honesty of purpose. He had grown painfully
sensible of his deficiencies, and it was almost
laughable to see with what diligence he strove
to repair them in his leisure evenings. The
manuals of popular information that he read, the
lists of sober facts that he committed to memory,
the instructive lectures that he attended, are

beyond the calculation of his biographer. Odds and ends of his undigested miscellaneous knowledge were continually bursting from him, like scraps from an over-full rag-bag, to the sly and secret amusement of his companions. Not one of them cared to laugh at him outright; for his good temper made him liked, and his romantic circumstances made him admired. Who does not, voluntarily or involuntarily, conceive a respect for the heir to ten thousand a-year?

For six months he remained in the lawyer's office, greatly improving both in mind and manner, as the conceit of himself was rubbed out of him by intimate contact with other young fellows wiser and cleverer than he. Then the question was proposed to him, whether he was willing to accede to his mother's wishes, and return home. But Francis George had not tasted the sweets of liberty in vain; he wrote an affectionately respectful letter to his mother, telling her he preferred to remain in London—in which decision his father secretly upheld him. Mrs. Percival Monke now began to lament her hasty banishment of her son, and would have been glad to recall him on almost any terms; but she was much too tenacious of her maternal authority to stoop to him and say so, therefore the breach between them widened. The sudden marriage of Flora Monke with a penniless ensign, utterly overthrowing her design for the reunion of Hardington and Frogholmes, exasperated her still more against her son; and, in the first bitterness of her disappointment, she indited to him the following letter :—

"Hardington, March 12, 182-.

"FRANCIS GEORGE,—

"You must have heard of your cousin Flora's elopement with Frederick Steele: thus you are answerable for her ruin as well as your own. I throw you off entirely now. You have acted the part of an undutiful and ungrateful son. You have taken from me the sole object for which I lived. Hardington and Frogholmes can never again be one; and you, cruel, indifferent, wicked, unworthy boy, are the sole cause. You need not trouble yourself to send me any more of your ill-spelt protestations of affection : I believe in deeds, not in words. From this day forth your existence is nothing to me. You must have Hardington when I die; but while I live, not a single sixpence shall you have. You may live where and how you can ; and the worst wish I wish you is, that if you live to have children of your own, they may wring your dearest feelings as cruelly as you have wrung mine. And so, I remain,

"Your injured and aggrieved mother,

"CECILY PERCIVAL MONKE."

Francis George showed the letter to his father, who only shrugged his shoulders, and wished his wife would give him his full discharge from Hardington also, though without curtailing his supplies ; but the young man dutifully endeavoured to soften her feelings towards him, and his failure was not chargeable on him.

"Woman's a riddle, indeed!" cried old Leatherhead, when his client wrote to him that she should henceforward stop her son's allowance, and that he must maintain himself independently of her. "Woman's not always a pleasant riddle either!"

Francis George would have had no difficulty

in raising money on his expectations had he been
so disposed; but, as old Leatherhead advised him
not, and gave him a reasonably liberal salary,
he resigned himself without difficulty to his fate:
resigned himself all the more readily, because
Mr. Proby had got a living a few miles from
town, and had brought his family to reside there.
Willie went down every Saturday and stayed
until Monday, and Francis George always made
him discourse about his father and mother, his
sisters and brothers, when he came back, until
Willie was tired of the subject.

"Come down, and see them yourself. I'm sure
you will be welcome," Willie suggested, one day;
and without any more formal invitation, Francis
George went.

VI.

WILLINGHAM PARSONAGE was a pretty spot, quite
rural, though almost within sight of London
smoke, and the young Probys flourished there
quite as well as they had ever done in the wilds
of Yorkshire—almost better. Katie happened to

be in the garden cutting flowers for the drawing-
room vases, when her brother and Francis George
arrived. She coloured up as beautifully as the
roses in her hand when her former lover bowed
low before her, and immediately proposed to go
and seek her mother; as no one gainsaid her,
away she flew. Mrs. Proby was sitting in her
work-room when her daughter ran in, laughing
but confused, with mischievous eyes and flushed
cheeks.

"Mamma, guess whom Willie has brought
home. I was never so startled in my life," she
cried, out of breath; "and I never saw anybody
so changed in a couple of years before!"

Mamma lowered her spectacles and looked out
of the window, where she saw her son and his
companion walking.

"Is it Francis George Percival Monke,
Katie?" she asked, puzzled.

"Yes, mamma, and so altered. Don't you
remember how foolish he was, and how we used
to laugh at him?"

"Hush, my dear, the window is open, and he
may hear you. I must go down and receive

him: but Willie should have let us know.
The best room must be got ready for him, I
suppose;" and Mrs. Proby laid aside spectacles
and thimble, and went down-stairs to welcome
her son's friend.

When Katie followed her, about ten minutes
after, it was in as sedate and composed a manner as she was capable of assuming on short
notice; but she could not prevent a bright and
rosy maidenly consciousness flickering in eye and
cheek as she faced Francis George. He blushed
too, and stammered a little when he began to
speak, exactly in his old way; which put her
at her ease more than anything else could have
done. He was very anxious to appear to his
best advantage before her, and to impress her
with a worthier opinion of his sense than she
used to have. He began to epitomize a very
solid lecture that he had heard a few evenings
before. He ought to have understood the smile
that curled about her pretty mouth better than
he did. Sharp-witted Katie understood him well
enough, and kind-hearted Katie did not fail to
encourage him to shine to the utmost; but she

thought his subject rather of the gravest to introduce five minutes after they met.

"You are becoming quite a scientific character, Francis George," was papa Proby's observation at dinner, when the young gentleman had made what he thought a very impressive display of his new learning. "It is really creditable to you to have acquired so much solid information."

Francis George felt so pleased, and glanced at Katie to see if he had elicited her approbation also. Katie smiled to conceal her temptation to laugh, and he was delighted. Most fluent did he become on every subject of interest in which he was sufficiently well up to speak correctly. Pictures, books of travels and biography, of poetry and romance, took their turn, until, if there was a doubt about what he knew, it was a doubt whether he did not know too much. Katie would have been glad to hear him discourse on everyday matters, but Francis George, with an old reputation to destroy and a new one to create, was not to be beguiled into trivialities. When he left Willingham early on Monday morning with Willie Proby, he left it in the pleasing consciousness that he had inspired everybody with respect for his learning.

" A well-informed young man," Mrs. Proby gravely admitted him to be.

" Not so dull as he was, either," said Katie.

" Out of evil good has come," observed the clergyman. " His banishment from Hardington turns out to be very beneficial."

" But it is a great shame, papa ! " cried Mistress Katie, firing up and looking very pretty ; " a great shame that his mother should have quarrelled with him because he would not marry Flora Monke: it would have been strange if he had liked her, I think, such a sarcastic girl as she was, and a flirt besides ! "

Papa Proby lifted his eyebrows, a little amazed, at his daughter's decision of speech ; and Katie, conscious that she had spoken rather harshly, blushed and became silent.

Francis George became a constant visitor at Willingham after this, and strove laboriously to win golden opinions from all the family. If his heavy talk bored them a little sometimes, they tried to forgive it ; and by and by, Katie could have offered evidence that he was capable of more interesting discourse when he had her ear alone. In the garden, for instance, up and down the pear-tree walk, does anybody think that while Francis George was speaking with so much whispered earnestness to Katie's curls that he was holding forth on interesting geological speculations? Would anybody credit that while Katie contemplated her shoe so so steadily, when they paused under the old yews, that she was meditating on the revolutions of heavenly bodies? Or does anybody imagine for a moment that when they sat so long in the little summer-house, they were trying to square the circle, or discussing the secret of perpetual motion? If anybody does, anybody is much mistaken.

"I think, mamma, I should be very happy with him," said Mistress Katie one day at her mother's knee. There had been an interview in papa Proby's study, and much talk, even more serious than scientific talk, and the daughter was making her confession. "I think, mamma, I should be very happy with him. I am sure he is very fond of me. He is a good, faithful fellow, mamma, or he would never have sought me out again, when he knows how I used to make fun of him, would he ? "

Mamma dare not undertake to say. "Katie must judge for herself ;" she added, "Katie was most capable of judging."

"But you think him good, mamma. You think his principles and temper are trustworthy ? "

"Yes, love, papa and I are quite satisfied on that head."

"Then, mamma, dear, why are you so cold and doubtful about us ? "

"Because, Katie, Hardington is in the way —his mother is in the way. Remember our difference of position."

"I wish he were never to be anything more than a lawyer's clerk," sighed Katie, getting off her knees and gliding to the window. Francis George was impatiently pacing the lawn, waiting for her reappearance, and in a minute or two Mrs. Proby was alone.

VII.

FRANCIS GEORGE PERCIVAL MONKE wrote to his mother, announcing his engagement to Katie Proby, and asking her consent to their marriage. No answer was returned. He wrote to her again. Mr. Proby wrote. Mrs. Proby wrote. Katie wrote. No answer. Francis George then addressed his father, and the now servile old gentleman wrote to him, that he was free to please himself. His mother was perfectly indifferent to all his proceedings. If he wanted to know whether she would do anything for him, her answer to that was—No.

So Francis George Percival Monke, heir of Hardington, lord of the manor of Hardington, married Katie Proby, and took her home to a little six-roomed suburban villa, and went on toiling as a lawyer's clerk; went on toiling through the best years of his life; went on toiling until four children had been born to him in the little six-roomed house; went on toiling until the present life in its affectionate simplicity had quite obliterated the hard lines of the former coldly ostentatious life; went on "toiling, rejoicing, sorrowing," until he had neither hope nor anticipation in the magnificent future which must come to him in the common course of nature.

There is plenty of space for happiness in a six-roomed suburban villa, with a garden of ten feet square—at least so the life of Francis George Percival Monke and Katie, his wife, testified. They had one care, and that was to give to their sons and daughters such an education as would pass them forward in the world easily: this care was their only one. And they had one sorrow— Katie's first-born died, and was laid to rest in Willingham churchyard.

But whatever their cares, whatever their sorrows, whatever their joys, they were all mutual, and served but to draw closer together the links of affection and friendship that united the husband and wife. Neither ever regretted for a moment any sacrifice that had to be made for the other's sake.

VIII.

IT is more than twenty years since the heir of Hardington and Katie were married. He has come to his kingdom at last, ripe in age, ripe in experience, and indifferent except to the best uses of his wealth, because he has learnt how little its superfluities can influence our actual happiness in life.

His mother said, before she died, that she forgave him, (forgave him what?) and sent for him to receive her blessing. Her son, who retained always his awe and respect for her, fancies himself the better for it—perhaps he is the better for it—I would not like to think that any kin of mine could carry an enmity against me into the other world. Whatever our wrongs, whatever our grievances, surely we can afford to lay them down with every other burden of life when we come to the grave-side!

There is a different rule in Hardington now from that which prevailed there once. Nowhere have the benefits of these times made themselves more felt than there.

From the Diary.

Mr. Dover returned from town last night, and late though he was, he came up at once to communicate his tidings. He has seen Harry, and Harry's wife, and Harry's baby, and Hannah proudly installed in charge of all three of them.

I am sure the account he brought was as good as a cordial to us, and gave me a better night's rest than I have enjoyed since the letter of confession came. Felix had left Emmy, Miss Bootle, and me, and had gone to his study after tea, so that when Mr. Dover arrived, he found us in the drawing-room alone, and we talked the affair over like a little knot of conspirators.

Harry had received his father's letter the morning his friend called, and was sensible of the wrong he had done towards us, but by no means repentant for his marriage; at which Mr. Dover says he is not surprised, for the little wife is altogether charming, beautiful, and intelligent, though very childlike and full of the timidity of inexperience.

Harry told him that she hugged Hannah, and began to cry for joy when she saw her, and heard she had gone to stay and take care of the baby, which is a capital little baby, but a dreadful anxiety to its parents. Mr. Dover said, altogether they looked very much like playing at being married and keeping house, but he was sure that Harry's wife had in her the making of an excellent woman; the Sunday he spent with them was her birthday, and he heard that she was only eighteen.

I was very anxious to hear of *her* connections, because *they* must have been cognizant of the marriage. Mr. Dover said Harry was not, at first, disposed to be communicative on the subject; but at last it oozed out that she was the ward of an old gentleman who had absolutely given his consent to the marriage, and not gainsaid its concealment.

Mr. Dover saw this singular guardian, and was pleased with him rather than otherwise. He is a bachelor, very absent in manner, but genuinely kind and good; in no profession, and living on small means, sentimental and romantic as a girl.

The young people are in lodgings not far from him, and they all look after each other. Harry's wife has no parents, and was an only child; she was quite without money, and this peculiar bachelor guardian had had her educated at a school where only six girls were taken, under the care of a sister of his own.

Harry met her the first time at the house of one of his college friends' father's where she was visiting, and after a rapid courtship of three months, they were married. She was his companion on his Welsh reading tour—much he read, I should think.

I feel quite buoyant again after the information that Mr. Dover brought. Harry's crime is one that will soon be forgiven and forgotten, since its consequences are so little likely to be bad. Emmy and I can hardly congratulate each other enough on what we have heard of the little wife.

I had a secret dread that she might be an inferior
girl with only a pretty face, and that Harry might
live bitterly to repent of his impetuosity; an
underbred, foolish woman is the worst companion
a man of education can be tied to. Perhaps
thoughtless Harry has been more lucky than he
quite deserved to be. Her name is Janet, and
the baby has been christened James Hertford,
after the queer bachelor guardian, its godfather.

While Mr. Dover was telling us what he had
seen and heard, and delivering his numerous
messages to Emmy, John brought word that his
master wanted to speak to the curate before he
left the house, so we sent him away to the library
at once, only too glad that his comfortable tidings
should be spread. Felix and he stayed talking
together so long that we women went to bed, but
Felix shows in the renewed cheerfulness of his
voice and manner, that he is relieved of his chief
anxiety about Harry.

Mr. Dover's eldest brother, a captain in the mer-
chant service, returned with him to spend Christ-

mas, and make Emmy's acquaintance. He called this morning, and we consider him a very frank, pleasant man. Belle and he struck up an alliance, and, with Steenic as guide, they have set off for a walk 'cross country to see the hounds meet at Bowerham gap.

How strangely glad one's heart feels after a season of trouble and fear, when the clouds lift, and one begins to perceive that things are not nearly so bad as might have been expected! I am as bright to-day as if Felix had withdrawn his veto on poor Harry's coming, and told us to expect him to-morrow. But there is no chance of that.

We were all cheerful enough, however, to listen to Miss Bootle's lively account of how she had been photographed, and to laugh as merrily as if dull care were not sitting at some of our hearts. She told us about it after tea, when Felix went to his study to revise his Christmas-day sermon.

HOW MISS BOOTLE WAS PHOTOGRAPHED.

In passing by Miss Wolsey's shop one morning, I perceived a frame full of likenesses hanging at the door-post. In the centre was the counterfeit presentment of Miss Wolsey herself, in all the crispness of Sunday silk gown and best cap ; two military officers flanked her on either side, Mr. Withers was over her head, and Mr. Dove below her feet, while four infantine groups occupied the angles.

So public an exposure of well-known characters surprised me. "Never, never," I said to myself, "would Lydia Bootle make her countenance the gazing-stock of a market-place ! " And, with rather more than my usual severity, I entered the bun-shop to ask what it all meant? Miss Wolsey did not allow me time to open my mouth, but said :

"The celebrated photographic artist, Mr. Buck,

is in the town, Miss Bootle. You must see him. You will be delighted."

I replied, " Oh, indeed ! "

This simple exclamation, with the tone I threw into it, immediately checked Miss Wolsey's vivacity. She saw I was slightly ruffled, and she endeavoured to propitiate me by adding:

" There is no harm in it, Miss Bootle. Many respectable people have been done."

" No harm !" I ejaculated,—" no harm ! when men in dignified professions, fathers of families (I alluded to Mr. Dove), allow themselves to be posted up on walls like sign-boards, or circus-bills ! Oh, Miss Wolsey ! " I have a respect for the woman, and I eyed her with a mild rebuke.

" I will have mine taken down, if you think it improper, Miss Bootle. I am sure I meant no offence to anybody," she said sadly.

I did not suffer the impression I had made to pass away, but rejoined sharply, " When you are a public character, Miss Wolsey, then be exhibited, and not before; " and I walked with a firm step out of the shop.

At the corner by the church, I encountered

Miss Parley, fresh from her early gossip.   " Have you been done, my dear?" she exclaimed, without exchanging the usual compliments;   "isn't it marvellous?"

I asked stiffly, what she meant?

" From two-and-sixpence upwards, single figures; and every additional figure one shilling extra," was her reply.   I wished her good morning; for she was in a gasping state of mental confusion, owing, probably, to an overfulness of news; and I walked on to Mr. Dove's.

Mrs. Dove was dressed to go out, with her tract-basket in her hand; and the two girls with their best hats, and baby in his feather and scarlet coat, were all undergoing a full parade examination previous to accompanying her.   I saw at once some great undertaking was contemplated.   Mrs. Dove is a favourite of mine. I knew her, an extremely pretty girl, before her marriage, and have always been in the habit of giving her advice about the training of her little ones (the eldest, Jenny Polly, is my godchild). Therefore I was not surprised when she exclaimed, grasping my hand in her cordial way :

"Dear Miss Lydia, I was just coming over to your house to consult you about the children's pictures. Must I have them done in a group, or singly? Miss Parley has given me such an account of Mr. Buck's skill in taking babies, that I was determined little Alfy should be done too."

"The whole town seems to have run mad about these photographs," I replied. "Do you like such portraits? For my part, I think them very displeasing. All those exposed outside the bun-shop look as black as ink."

"Miss Parley said they were exquisite, and Mr. Dove was done yesterday. Go with us, Miss Lydia, and you will see. Miss Parley will be waiting for us there now, by this time. I told her to go and prepare Mr. Buck for the arrival of a party," said Mrs. Dove.

I consented.

The photographic apparatus was set up in Miss Wolsey's garden, a bit of ground about sixteen feet square. It consisted of a lofty board over which was stretched a white sheet; a kitchen-chair stood with its back to it, and, close by, a circular deal-table covered with a crochet-work

anti-macassar. Opposite, was a machine supported on a sort of mahogany scaffold. It had
one large round glass eye, with a huge black
patch of cotton velvet hanging over it. I had
never seen anything of the kind before; but, as
I never display my ignorance except when I
cannot help it, I looked round reflectively, and
was silent. Not so the youthful Doves, who,
Mr. Buck remarked, were not at all in a photographic humour; for they capered about like
dancing-dolls, instead of being quite still. In
one corner of the garden was a dejected plum-
tree; and, on a bench beneath it, were two bee-
hives, with all the bees in full buzz. Alfy
wanted to touch them, and screamed for a full-
sized bumble-bee that had settled on Mr. Buck's
bottle of what Miss Parley called " the chemicals,"
until his distracted nurse pacified him with a
bun, while Jenny Polly and Lucy tugged at
their mamma's skirts or made her the centre of
a merry-go-round, and refused to be caught, to
be inducted into the chair.

I perceived that somebody must take an initia-
tory step, for the artist stood looking gloomily

bewildered in the confusion; therefore I went forward, announced that I would be done the first, and took my seat in the chair. I felt a curiosity to see my own features portrayed; for, though I have reached the seventh age of woman, I had never before been taken in any style.

The preparatory expectation was almost as bad as the agonizing moments spent in a dentist's parlour, after you have received the pleasing intelligence that he is engaged, but will attend to you in five minutes. Mr. Buck shut himself up in what I have every reason to believe was Miss Wolsey's coal-cellar; while, under Miss Parley's direction, I composed myself into an attitude: the left hand on my waist, the right resting gracefully on the anti-macassar. The artist soon reappeared, and performed certain mysterious evolutions, which Miss Parley said was focussing me. When I was focussed, he looked at me very intently, and said, "Now, ma'am, fix your eyes on this tree-trunk, and do not move them in the least: now!"

I do not mind confessing that I expected a flash, as of lightning, to burst upon my face when the great black velvet patch was temporarily removed from the awful glass eye, and I immediately screwed up both my own eyes to avoid it.

"Tish!" cried Mr. Buck, impatiently, "we must try again!" And he disappeared into the coal-cellar once more.

Mrs. Dove and Miss Parley both immediately began to give me instructions how to behave. The first said, "There is nothing to be afraid of, dear Miss Lydia; do keep your eyes open the next time!" "And," added Miss Parley, "do not look so severe. Say 'plum!' It composes the features into such an amiable expression— 'plum!'"

So I said "plum," and felt that I looked idiotic; and everybody else said "plum," to show me its dulcifying effect on the countenance. Mr. Buck reappeared; and, this time, with a strong effort I did keep my eyes steady, and was profoundly astonished that nothing alarming or unpleasant occurred. The artist rushed into the cellar again, and Miss Parley explained, that he had gone thither to develop me. Dear me, I was never developed before! My pulse quickened.

I believe everybody is anxious to see how they
look in their portrait, and I quite held my breath
when Mr. Buck came out of his retirement and
exhibited mine.

"Oh! you are quite flattered; but it is an
admirable likeness! Oh, admirable!" cried Miss
Parley.

"It is very good; the dress has taken so well,"
added Mrs. Dove. My dress was a black and
red silk plaid: I like a striking pattern and full
colour.

"It is indeed a faithful miniature of my face:
it gives even the slight obliquity of my nasal
feature, the bumpiness of my forehead, and the
steady fulness of my dark grey eye; but I did
not agree with Miss Parley in considering it too
favourable. No: photography is not a flatterer."

Jenny Polly, seeing that I had come out of the
ordeal uninjured, now consented to be put into
position on the chair; but no amount of per-
suasion could induce her to sit still when there,
and, after five failures, she was permitted to stand
down, and her mamma undertook to show her
how easy it was to sit still and be good; but, at

the critical moment, turning her head to say, "You see, Jenny Polly, how quiet I can be," the result was that she was represented with two faces.

"Nothing remarkable in that!" whispered Miss Parley, who never lost the opportunity of saying an ill-natured thing, whether true or false.

The three children were next arranged in a group, and the issue was general confusion; we exhausted ourselves with devices to fix their attention, but all in vain.

I pitied Mr. Buck. He was a little old man, with a wild shock of black hair, beard and moustache, and a pair of irascible blue eyes. He wore a blouse of dark cloth belted round his person with a broad band of patent leather, and evidently considered himself very picturesque. He was hot and moist, and his hands were spotted and stained with the chemicals, and his face likewise. Altogether, he looked as if he would have been much the better for a plunge into the water-butt —which occupied a large angle of the little garden—both as to cleanliness and coolness. I was growing tired, and anxious to be away, for the bees, aggravated by our noisy invasion of their territory, showed stinging propensities and buzzed quite savagely. Deeply disappointed, Mrs. Dove proposed to pay and go, when Miss Parley said she should like to be done herself for half-a-crown; and Mr. Buck immediately focussed her. She seemed much agitated, and expressed astonishment at the firmness with which I had sustained myself through the trying operation; but kept herself, nevertheless, as still as a statue.

"We shall do," said Mr. Buck, triumphantly, as he issued from the coal-cellar after the developing process; and indeed the portrait he exhibited was a perfect success.

"But it is not a pretty likeness," said Miss Parley, plaintively—"not at all a pretty likeness. Will you try again?"

Mr. Buck protruded his nether lip slightly, and said, if she desired it, he would; but that it was not likely he should obtain a better. "It is yourself, ma'am—your very self!" he observed.

When I mention that Miss Parley has a high colour, chiefly concentrated in her thin, peaked nose, and a drooping eyelid, it will be seen at once how great were the difficulties in the artist's way: she varied her position the next time, so as to hide the latter defect, but was still dissatisfied. I know Mr. Buck said something worse than " Tish ! " as he plunged into the coal-cellar once more; for his voice was quite rasped when he came out and desired her to fall into position again. It will scarcely be credited that this foolish woman caused Mr. Buck to do her *eight* several times in *eight* different attitudes ; indeed she did not desist until there was nothing left to take but a back view, and then she paid her half-crown with a grudge. I was astonished at her meanness; and to see her hesitation over those eight portraits, as to which she should have finished and framed, was ludicrous. After taking and rejecting everybody's advice, she ended by keeping the first, which was certainly the best.

" After all, Miss Lydia, I would rather have mine than yours," she said to me, as we were talking the matter over in the bun-shop; " you know it was *portraits*, not *pictures*, we went for, and it is easy to buy a fancy engraving. I am glad mine is a true likeness; I never consider people *really respect us* when they *flatter* either in words or *deeds ;* and Mr. Buck has flattered you out of recognition."

I was silent. Miss Parley was evidently mortified, by the way she emphasized her remarks, and it was of no use to aggravate her further; but Miss Wolsey, for the sake of the artist's credit, perhaps, took upon herself the reply.

" Flattery, Miss Parley? there cannot be such a thing in photography : Mr. Buck explained to me the whole process. People complain sometimes that it makes them uglier, but I never heard of anybody being made prettier."

" Just come and look, then—if you can tell Miss Bootle's likeness you have better eyes than I can pretend to have ! " retorted Miss Parley; and she led the way back to the garden; all of us following in a body.

When Mr. Buck saw us, he put his hands up to his head, and grasped his hair frantically; but was pacified when Miss Wolsey explained why we had returned, and he brought the portraits forth. Miss Parley took mine sharply out of his hand, and began to hold forth on its de-

merits; when suddenly a bee settled on her wrist
and stung her severely. She gave out a shrill
cry, and dropped my pretty little effigy upon the
gravel, where it was utterly obliterated and destroyed. Mr. Buck ejaculated his little word
again, retired into the coal-cellar abruptly, and
did not come forth while we stayed. Miss Parley
feigned deep regret, but I am sure she went away
in a better and more contented frame of mind than
she would have done but for the happy accident.

"I will tell you where the fault lay, dear,"
she said, as we parted at Saint Mary's corner;
"it made you look too young. You seemed like
a handsome person of fifty, or thereabouts; and
you know you are much more than that; for I
recollect you quite a young woman when I was
a little chit at Miss Thoroton's school. Don't you
recollect asking me to dinner once, when I came
in a white frock and blue sash, and we had lamb
and asparagus, and gooseberry-tart with cream
after?"

I did remember that time: it was when Mr.
Fenton was curate of Saint Mary's. He dined
at our house the same day, and little Judith

Parley clung close to my elbow all the evening, and listened to every word that we said.

The next day I perceived that one of the military gentleman's portraits had given place to Miss Parley's; and there she hung for a week or more, in full view of the market people. I went as usual for my luncheon-bun, after doing my Saturday purchases in country produce; and, while eating it by the counter, I heard the butcher's boy (Mr. Steele's, not Mr. Edgebone's boy) call out to one of his acquaintance, "My eye, Tom! if here isn't old Miss Parley. What a stunning guy she looks! don't she?"

And I fear Miss Parley heard also; for she entered a moment after, excessively red, and immediately went into a tirade upon the lowness, the coarseness, and the stupidity of the common people.

www.ingramcontent.com/pod-product-compliance
Lightning Source LLC
Chambersburg PA
CBHW060539030726
47498CB00004B/1253